Schoolgirl Chums

By the same author

St Ursula's in Danger

ST. URSULA'S

Schoolgirl Chums

Peter Glidewell

DRAGON
Granada Publishing

Dragon Books
Granada Publishing Ltd.
8 Grafton Street, London W1X 3LA

Published by Dragon Books 1983

British Library Cataloguing in Publication Data
Glidewell, Peter
Schoolgirl chums.—(St Ursula's)
I. Title   II. Series
823'.914 [J]   PZ7

ISBN 0-583-30683-7

Reproduced, printed and bound in Great Britain by
Hazell Watson & Viney Limited,
Member of the BPCC Group,
Aylesbury, Bucks

Set in Plantin

'. . . Daddy it really is the end of my first term here. Tomorrow there's the carol service and then all the other girls go home. I suppose I should be feeling really Christmassy. In fact, I'm rather miz . . .'

To an observer, this 'mizness' might have seemed curious, since the fire in the grate crackled quite cheerfully, and, though the wind moaned in the chimney, pieces of holly were gleaming brightly all over the oak panelled walls. Indeed, even the snowy scene outside the windows might have been designed simply to emphasize the warmth within the cosy fourth form common room of St Ursula's School for Girls. But as Alison bent again to her task, she had no eyes for the snow, or the holly either. This pen, flying across the page might have been her one and only interest in life.

'Of course I understand about your mission and everything having to be top secret; but now the last day's arrived and still no word from you. Daddy, I'm worried . . . I can't deny it. Oh Daddy you promised . . . You promised to be back in time.' And Alison shed one . . . no . . . two tears.

This time they splashed right down on to the page and she had to screw up the paper, just in case her father ever *did* come to read it. 'What a little pig you are,' she told herself, angrily wiping the corner of her eye with her fist. 'How could anyone feel so sorry for herself, after all that . . . *unbelieveableness?*'

They were singing carols in the next room. She listened for a while, pen in mouth, to the cheery girlish voices uplifted in song. Christmas in school wouldn't be so bad . . . really quite novel if you thought about it; a Christmas spent with cook and

Mr Brisling and the school dog. She smiled, in spite of everything. At least she'd have Miss Devine to herself.

And at that, her heart gave a little bound, her thoughts racing right back to three months ago . . . to the late afternoon sunshine and the click of croquet balls on a wide expanse of the smoothest lawn in south Dorset.

CHAPTER
1

'Come on. Your shot.'

Colonel Dayne's smooth military voice could be heard, ringing out from those mists of memory, with its usual no-nonsense tone. Alison jumped. It was a crispness he usually reserved for the polo ground.

'Sorry.'

Mallet was applied, and a ball was hit rather half heartedly through a hoop.

'Feeling a bit gloomy?'

The voice had lowered a notch and the eyes under the hand that shaded them from the evening sun watched her anxiously.

Alison and her father were playing croquet and the father whom she loved was beating her as usual.

'Just a bit,' she admitted . . . 'having to leave all this . . . and you. Daddy, I realize you can't say where you're going but won't we be able to exchange any letters at all?'

'Too risky girlie. Honestly I mean that. They might be intercepted.' It was true she supposed. Over the years, she'd had to adapt to such aspects of her father's work. For the Colonel was a member of the British Secret Service. 'Tell you what,' he laughed. 'Why don't you write me a log instead?'

'If you mean a *diary*,' Alison sighed, 'why don't you say so?'

'I do. I do mean a diary. Write a diary about everything that happens. There'll be so much going on. Just wait till you're clouting the pill across the hockey field,' he promised, whamming his own pill now into her own, and then, after the last humiliating croquet, smacking it hard against the winning post. He grinned like a boy, satisfied with his win. For Alison it was the end of another game; one she'd played with him willingly all her life. They'd been everywhere together; India, Palestine, Africa. It was hard now to think they were to be separated from each other.

As they strolled together towards the open french windows, she must have shown it. For the eyes in the weather beaten face softened. They were eyes that took in everything. Of course he was finding it as difficult as she, to be cheerful. Sometimes, in his soldierly way he found it hard to express his feelings.

'Don't fret my little girl.' His hand stole into hers. 'You'll like it at St Ursula's, never fear. It's ridiculously lovely there.' His voice was eager, anxious to console. 'The building's so much older than this place . . . There's even a secret passage.'

And Alison's big grey eyes opened wide. For in spite of herself, she knew this was something she could *not* ignore. They stopped walking.

'You're making it up,' she laughed.

'No I'm not. Promise. Leads out of the Old Girls' Dormitory. You press a hidden button in the panelling, then lo and behold, the whole affair slides back. Oh, come on. Things won't be so bad. St Ursula's is a darn fine school . . . and as for the Headmistress, Miss Devine . . . well . . .'

Alison really dissolved in mirth at last, half joy, half tears.

She went up and leaned on him, burying her head in that familiar smell.

'Oh Daddy, you're so funny. I've heard all this before. You like her rather a lot, don't you?'

And as she gazed into his face, her eyes twinkling, she felt protective towards him again. If he'd been wearing one, she'd have straightened his tie. Goodness . . . he was more worried about her going to school than *she* was.

'Darned attractive certainly.' He smiled, then kicked his ball away across the grass. 'Though pretty strict mind. I told her clearly what a young savage she'd have on her hands . . . your Mama long dead and me away so much of the time . . .'

This was *too* much.

'Daddy; you're an ass.'

The girl turned away, smothering her hilarity. A grown up could sometimes be so ridiculous; more awkward even than a shy young horse. At this moment she felt a need to be alone with someone who viewed life more simply.

Although invisible on the other side of the tree, old Nutkin would be grazing in the favourite corner of his paddock, peacefully unaware of the imminent changes in his life. It was the only way to feel, she knew that clearly as for the last time she threw her arms round the shaggy neck, forcing the black eyes for a moment to look into hers. Here was a puzzle.

When you needed them most, then it was that you realized these animals didn't need *you* after all. Thus comes the first lesson of the stoic. And thus, as she kissed the long suffering and patient face, she found herself gazing into quite different lenses . . . in fact a pair of binoculars.

Otherwise almost hidden behind the paddock hedge the man waited, unflinching, motionless. He remained until angrily Alison started across the uneven ground to intercept. Then he bobbed out of sight.

When she reached the hedge, he had completely disappeared.

CHAPTER
2

'I say. Is that your father? He's rather ripping; and what a super row of ribbons.'

The voice was a girl's. It belonged to a fairly stocky little person, about her own age who was wearing the same grey and red school uniform as she wore herself, and possessed the frankest, jolliest, cheeriest face she had ever seen.

Alison and Colonel Dayne had left for the station at nine, travelling in the trap with Nutkin between the shafts. The morning struck cool, with the sky unexpectedly low and still, and a pall of grey cloud hanging menacingly over the hills.

Only two cars passed them on the country road that morning and both were foreign. It happened where the lane ran between high banks of ochre coloured sandstone, with the way consequently constricted. Identical black limousines, they had squeezed past so rudely as to bring cries of wrath to the hoary lips of Jones, the aged groom. 'Road hogs!'

The cloud of dust settled all over their clothes. Nutkin shied, almost breaking the traces, and it was some moments before order was restored. In thoughtful mood, the Colonel seemed content to brush himself down without comment and they drove on as quickly as possible.

Coming into the station yard at a brisk trot, Alison saw several cars drawn up, but none with foreign number plates. She jumped down immediately and began to haul at her bags.

'You leave that there to me Missy. You'll be fed up enough with 'em afore the day's out I'll be bound.' And they had left the old man to it.

Just as she thought they'd escaped, the two cars arrived with a squeal of brakes. Alison's heart sank.

'Oh Lord,' she whispered. 'Not *this* ghastly charade all over again . . .' They walked into the booking hall. Her father thoughtfully rubbed his chin. It was a sure sign of trouble and Alison felt a mounting irritation. 'Are you expecting something to happen?' she asked him closely. '*Are* you?'

For this was nothing new. They'd been through the same routine so many times. She'd never get used to it; not ever; and every time she prayed for it to be different. Let it be different this time.

They'd arrived at the ticket window. For a moment the Colonel stiffened as he caught sight of something across the railway line. Then a train had slid by, cutting off from view whatever it might have been there on the other platform.

The clanking locomotive filled the scene with noise and steam and the Colonel had to raise his voice above the banging of doors and porters yelling. 'A single to Cottley for my daughter and single to London for me . . . first class.' In full dress uniform, he too was to be a rail traveller that day. He was on his way to the Ministry, on very official business indeed. When she had told him about her man with the binoculars, he'd said 'hmmp'. Merely that. Not 'hurrummmmp' or even 'oh yes?'

More trouble in the Balkans proclaimed a newspaper hoarding.

Though a string of passengers waited to get on to the platform, at the barrier her father hung back. 'You toddle across girlie,' he said, easing her past the barrier, 'I won't be a minute.' And then through the clouds of steam she saw her.

The first thing that got you were her eyes. They were deeply, coolly, penetratingly blue, the sort that, when they moved, sent shivers down your spine. And as she spoke, the girl in the grey school uniform seemed cooler than cream herself, with her tip-tilted mouth and rose petal fresh complexion. Leaning nonchalantly from a carriage window she had looked Alison up and down, just once, from the soles of her shoes to the top of her round school hat before launching into:

'I say, you're new aren't you? Is that your father? He's rather ripping . . . and what a super row of ribbons.'

The carriage door had swung open then, and as Alison

clambered aboard from the bustle of the station, she was looking over her shoulder. Oh, she would so hate to miss him now . . . Although Alison had only half listened, and therefore failed to reply to the compliments, the other girl seemed quite unperturbed.

'Oh yes,' Alison managed absently to agree; and if she still kept her father in her field of vision, could it be because she was worried about his physical safety? She tried hard to quieten what was threatening to become panic. And when she finally turned to her new companion, it was with an almost fretful smile.

'He's got plenty of medals. And the VC.'

'Golly.' The reply sounded unnaturally easy and casual. 'My Dad's only a clergyman. Well . . . I say only. He's a Bishop actually. Isn't it awful him having such a scapegrace for a daughter?' She giggled complacently. 'Miss Prosser our second mistress is always saying to me . . . "I wonder what your father the Bishop would think of your conduct?"' Blonde head bobbing, the irrepressible child had given a fair imitation of her mistress's voice. 'She doesn't know Dad,' she prattled on, 'or she wouldn't talk in that stupid way. Now Miss Devine . . .'

The Colonel was at last approaching. He clutched a round box. Alison murmured, her attention only half on her companion. 'Oh yes. What about Miss Devine? Is she nice?'

'Nice? My dear, she's positive heaven.'

And now here was her father, a cloud of steam dividing them as he prepared to hand over an unnecessarily large box of chocolates.

'Ho ho, there you are. Did I see two school hats? I thought I did . . .' (He peered through the steam.)

'Hilary Marchant.' The blonde girl had stuck out her hand. She then leaned back as if in triumph.

'How d'ye do Hilary?' The Colonel emitted a throaty chuckle. 'Perhaps you'd be good enough to show my little girl the ropes?'

Gosh . . . he could be irritating at times. (It sounded as if there were already some private joke about her, between the two of them.) She protested: 'I'm not your "little girl" Daddy. I'm nearly fifteen.'

12

Amidst the press of passengers behind the barrier opposite, she had noticed two dark coated men. Dark spectacled, dark hatted, they had shouldered their way to the bars and now, like sullen animals, gazed unflinchingly across the platform.

With his back to them, the Colonel could not see these men. Should she warn him? She could not. She was paralysed, waiting for the action to begin. The Colonel handed over the chocs. His hand rested momentarily on hers.

'I know. I know,' he murmured soothingly.

At that moment came the flash.

That it was from a camera rather than from a gun came more as a surprise than a relief. Alison gaped.

The Colonel's reaction had been but to half incline his head, and now he was simply burbling on again, telling her about life and wasting precious love time, as though just to fill in the minutes.

'Remember what I said. You're bound to find school very different from home, but . . .'

'Persevere' . . . she muttered with him. It was always . . . 'persevere'.

'I s'pose,' he went on, 'school's rather like the army.' And he grinned. 'You may not like your officers . . . I'm sure heaps of my subalterns find me a terror . . . but it's your duty as one of the rank and file to obey orders.'

They'd not moved a muscle since the flash, those foul and toadlike creatures by the barrier. If it was only his photograph they wanted, why were they still hanging around? Perhaps waiting for the full face view he seemed determined not to give them. Oh, don't let them try to kill him, this rash and daredevil army man who was the only father she'd ever had . . . The guard was waving his flag and blowing his whistle. Alison felt her stomach squeeze tight. She had to choke to hold back the tears. This was it. This was the moment for her father's voice to lift, ready for the last homily. It came:

'If you get into a scrape, own up and take the consequences.'

There was a creak from the wheels. The whole long train was suddenly free, released into latent motion.

'Above all,' he shouted, 'never never tell a lie.'

What about 'I love you?' her heart screamed.

He was walking beside the moving train and they should

have been hugging for dear life but the train was sliding along, spiriting him away from her, taking those clinging hands and touching fingers. She cried out:

'You'll be back by Christmas; you will Daddy; you will. You promised.'

He had stopped walking and his voice came back crisp and clear. 'I'll be in touch as soon as I can.'

Behind the lonely waving figure, the two men walked on to the platform, stolidly, sullenly approaching his back. Then the train swung round a bend and he was out of sight.

CHAPTER 3

How can words describe the first numbing shock of being abandoned in a hostile world?

Alison stood for a while in her corner by the door, holding on to herself and gazing at the rocking floor.

'Going to school, the cab's at the door . . .
Little Jemima is crying once more . . .'

The silly words came from a song learned from an adored mother. However babyish, they were strong enough to bring yet another wave of nausea.

'You are ridiculous Alison Dayne,' she told herself sternly. 'How *can* you be alone with so many other folk?' Indeed everywhere she looked, there seemed to be bouncing, squealing girls, all in identical school macs, blazers and hats, yet underneath, presumably all different. Even now, as she went to the corner of this railway coach to gaze down the corridor, she spotted one familiar face.

It was a face, changed from a moment ago, now under some strain . . . its owner battling with a siege of smaller girls outside a compartment door. Enthusiastically arguing the point, this Hilary girl with flying blonde locks, struggled in combat.

Alison for the moment decided to put her cares away, and clutching her box of chocolates, approached.

'Hello,' gasped her erstwhile companion between bumps, 'seen a ghost?'

With hat squashed over one eye, her question had had a sharpish edge. Even allowing for such conditions of stress, the voice did not sound at all like the one she had just heard talking to her father. Yet she *looked* the same.

15

'No,' replied Alison cautiously. 'I just wondered what you were doing?'

'Keeping the self to the self you understand,' (gasp) . . . 'as we fourth formers can.' Bang. Thump.

'I bagged that seat first,' shrilled a small adversary with determination, 'and I'm having it.'

'Oh no you're not.'

'Ow . . . you're hurting me actually.'

'I'm meant to be hurting you baby dear. You're a nasty rowdy little toad.' The words emerged in short gasps.

'Can't you stuff a hatband in the odd mouth?' came another languid voice.

'Wouldn't even waste a hatband!'

The train rattled over some points, and from the swinging corridor the smaller girl found herself hurled into the adjacent compartment. This new version of Hilary wiped her hands with satisfaction.

'You've no right to interfere with us Jennifer Soames,' came the final riposte from the smaller girl. 'You're not in the fifth form yet. In fact you've only just arrived in the fourth.'

The door slammed to.

'*Jennifer*?' Alison enquired involuntarily.

'Yep. Got to be cruel to be kind don't you know . . . or they get ideas above their station. That was all for *you* you understand. Inside. Hilary's saved you a place.'

And Alison found herself being propelled. It was quite nice to be propelled. It was quite nice to be considered at all, yet the problem still remained unanswered.

'All right. So what d'you think we are?'

Two pink complexioned, two short bob haired profiles gazed at her with such earnest and cheerful enquiry, that she could not help feeling a surge of happiness and pleasure. For really, now she saw they were *not* the same, she knew she still had to pretend, if only to keep them happy.

So obediently she said: 'You're not *twins*?' And as they looked at each other, the corners of their mouths lifted in triumph.

'Quite right old thing . . . we're not . . . though we look the same . . .'

'Speak the same.'

'Devour the same chocolates.'

'And several other foods.'

'But mainly chocolates, especially ones like those. Park yourself dear girl.'

The school train, swaying momentarily as it rattled through some country station, jerked her case into its very best position on the rack. Then Alison plumped down.

'I didn't even thank my dad for these,' she laughed shakily, undoing the chocolates then lifting the lid.

'Heat of the moment, old bruised heart. He'd understand . . .'

'Good Heavens,' gasped Hilary. *What's that*?'

A chocolate had been removed. In its place in the very centre of this most expensive selection lay a little gold ornamental box. Alison stared. In that unnerving moment, her thoughts went buffeting straight back to her father and his queerness on the railway platform. That ingenuous face, those empty words of advice . . . she'd been aware that both had been made under the closest scrutiny for they were both being watched. But only now did it become clear why he'd failed to say a proper goodbye. As she peered mesmerised at the little object, its menace palpably grew, before her very eyes. She looked hopelessly at her friends, then back at the box.

Perhaps she suffered from an overactive imagination. Nevertheless it seemed, at that very moment, that an evil force was reaching out to clutch her throat. It was all she could do to resist twisting away her head. How far would they go, the people of this foreign land? How far would they *come*? Evidently a mystery would now be tormenting those sinister stolid people. *She* held the key to that mystery . . . or at least the responsiblity, for there was no apparent way of opening the little gold object. Would *they* realize what she had in her keeping and follow her to the ends of the earth? . . . or at least to St Ursula's School for Girls? It was a question to which there could be no definite answer. What a way to start a school career!

She felt poised between panic and disbelief.

Relieved that whatever the box contained was being carried every moment further from his enemies, would the Colonel, on the other hand, at this very moment be experiencing a certain smug satisfaction? No. She decided to give him the benefit of the doubt. It had been a reckless act, made on the spur of the moment. Now he'd be regretting his foolishness.

Always a gambler, he knew that, without taking chances, there could never be any real coup in his dangerous world. That was all right for him. He could run around the globe, free as air. She would be trapped in school. Alison drew in breath. She would guard this thing with her life. But even now she barely dared look round . . . lest she see a murderous slit eyed face . . . peering at her through the carriage window.

'Family heirloom, what?' Jennifer decided at last.

Lifting the heavy metal object, Alison weighed it in her hand.

They expected her to explain *something*.

'Seems to be locked,' she remarked boringly . . . 'but there's no key.'

'Obviously intended as a surprise gift.'

Hilary provided the answer to the puzzler with a finality that closed the case. Slipping the object in her pocket, Alison pushed the matter from her mind and the chocolates towards her new friends.

'Mm. Scrumptious.' Fingers poised over the goodies, Hilary glanced significantly at her old comrade in arms. 'Good to be getting back, eh old thing?'

'Ra-ther,' Jennifer agreed, popping a choc into her mouth. And they both beamed at Alison.

And at least, with that sealing gesture, a new friendship seemed to have begun.

As a little girl of six, Alison had once been taken by her governess to the home of an old friend of her father, a rather witchy person, living on the top of a hill.

In a gabled house at the end of a street of cobbles, the old lady, seated in a sedan chair, watched passers by through windows of green bottle glass. These were panes that made people come and go in a jerky way, distorting their faces so as to make them huge with popping eyes, or small enough to disappear into a pin. And Alison had sat transfixed for hours.

There had been other fascinations in that room; so many things to feel and see. There was silver plate behind locked glass doors. There were ornaments, flowers and dolls. Stuffed birds sat on the mantelpiece; a crystal ball on the sideboard. Above all there had been the books – shelves and shelves of them ranged all the way to the ceiling. Some were too large even to pick up, some small enough to slide under a door; most of them were out of reach and hardly any were for children. But what made up for *that* were the volumes on the bottom shelf. Here was a whole row of leather bound volumes, all the same size and all heavily embossed with the raised crests of antique gold she found so fascinating to touch.

And as, sandwiched by the squashed in comfort of her two new friends on the bouncing back row of the grey-green school bus, Alison handled the gold box, sliding its smoothness against the slippery mac pocket . . . there came once again the familiar feeling of a certain ribbed surface. This was the *same crest*. There was embossed on the lid of that heavy little box . . . a crown of gold.

The bus was turning into the drive and Alison sat up. She

19

craned eagerly for a first glimpse of her new home and her heart beat faster. Suddenly, there was the school, an old grey building, its windows afire in the evening sunshine. Down the drive the bus trundled, finally scrunching round in the gravel to halt outside the weatherbeaten door of metal studded oak.

And then, in a squeal of girls, they descended. In a whirl of waving hockey sticks, old friendships were being renewed and new ones begun. Girls were everywhere. They banged into Mr Brisling the crabbed old porter, who responded with cries of wrath. They ran hither and thither with such idiotic expressions of joy, you might have thought school the happiest place on earth. Alison joined in the throng surging into the porch.

'How ripping,' laughed Hilary. 'You're in the same dormy as Jen and me. Might as well go up now and bag a bed. Though hang on a mo. There's Enid with the hockey fixtures. Better check she hasn't made a complete ass of herself, and left me out altogether. It'd be just like her . . .' Hilary darted off.

Detached and wandering aimlessly towards some stairs, Alison found herself intercepted. A plain girl with plaits and large spectacles stuck on the end of a prominent red nose had approached so silently as to give her quite a shock.

'Excuse me,' this girl enquired, in a flat northern voice, 'but are you going to Nightingale Dormitory?'

'Yes.'

'You couldn't take me could you?' This unlikely person spoke in a downcast tone. 'I don't know the way.'

'Nor do I.' Alison intercepted a passing child. 'Sorry. But d'*you* know the way to Nightingale Dormitory?'

'Up there . . . first on the right.'

'Oh thanks.'

The girl watched. As the two mounted the old creaking wooden stair, there came the cool observation:

'You're not really allowed there during the day.' It was with the satisfaction of a reprimand duly delivered that she added before turning away: 'But I expect it's all right since you're new.'

'What a cheek! Who the heck does she think she is, bossy thing?' muttered the bespectacled girl. 'Did you want to come to this school?'

'Not particularly.'

'Nor me. I took the examination.'

'And presumably passed,' murmured Alison. They had reached the landing at the top of the stairs. From the wall the faded features of a grand Elizabethan lady gazed down on them. 'You must be frightfully clever.'

'Yes,' the other girl agreed simply, 'I am.'

'Goodness,' thought Alison to herself, unused to such frankness as they clattered down a linoleum covered passage ... 'Nothing could be plainer than that.'

And now here at last was the dorm, the word Nightingale written on the door in bright green paint. It was a medium sized polished room, seven beds on the sort of slidey floor that reminded you of hospitals.

Another girl was laying out clothes on her bed. She entirely ignored them. Frankly irritated by the aloofness, Alison felt no one should be too busy even to say hello. But about to introduce herself she caught sight of the expression on the face of the new acquaintance from the northern shires.

'Is this really where we sleep?' the other new girl wailed incredulously. 'I don't want to sleep with a whole lot of other people ... I want to go home.' The face that gazed upward so pathetically had become suddenly coursed with tears. It had been almost like turning on a tap. Perhaps she could do it to order?

'Oh, but you can't,' Alison hastened to answer. 'They won't let you.'

'Oh ... oh,' moaned the girl with increasing passion. 'Whatever am I going to do?'

'Stick it out like anyone else,' Alison was about to reply. But at that moment Hilary burst into the room like a warm wind from the south.

'Hurry up. Tea's in a jiff.' Spotting the weeping one at a glance she said, 'Hello? What's the matter with her?' Twisting the heaving shoulders round to face her, she pronounced loftily: 'Oh ... new girl,' as though this explained everything. 'I should leave her alone. She'll get over it.'

'But Hilary,' Alison protested, not having been at school long enough to blunt finer feelings quite so callously, 'she's terrified. Can't you see?'

'Don't go. Don't leave me,' came more sobs.

Hilary pulled a face, then speaking in raised tones as though to a deaf cretin shouted: 'Don't you want any tea?'

Vehemently the girl shook her head. Flinging herself full length upon the hard narrow bed, she wept bitterly.

'I'll be along in a minute,' Alison said. She sat on the bed next to the prone, weeping figure. Hilary turned on her heel.

'You're mad actually. Lots of them are like this at first. And Prosey gets awfully ratty if we're late in.'

Prosey's rattiness was something Alison had not yet experienced. And anyway there was another reason for remaining. Having spotted her own bed, it was the work of a moment to take the little gold box from her pocket and slide it under her pillow. The snivelling one was too busy snivelling to notice; but Alison felt as worried as a squirrel over a nut. The hiding place was not satisfactory. At the moment she could think of nowhere else. A quick reconnaissance of the otherwise now deserted dormy and its floor, moreover, revealed no nook nor even a cranny to hide such a considerable item.

She remained to deliver a few more words of comfort, then with foreboding went down to eat. For a long time she could not find the place. But then the telltale clatter of knives and forks led her to the refectory.

Ranged in a square round one lonely central table, seemingly innumerable girls sat at tea. It was a singular arrangement and one that immediately struck a note of panic. For enclosed there in the very centre sat an erect iron grey woman, slowly and disagreeably masticating a thin wedge of currant slice.

At Alison's timorous appearance, a pair of eyelids fluttered for a moment behind lenses. Then the full accusatory gaze of disbelief was unleashed on her.

'And who are you may I ask?'

All faces turned. Crimson shame spread to the roots of the latecomer's hair.

'Alison Dayne.'

'Indeed?'

It was not the sarcasm so much as the satisfaction that made the voice the most unpleasant Alison had ever heard. Revolving slowly, as on a pivot, the mistress turned to her flock.

'So nice to know Miss Dayne deigns to honour us with her presence. Do you always come in so late to tea at school?'

'I've never been to school before. I've always had a tutor at home.'

'Good Heavens!'

That they had evoked only the faintest of titters suggested that, after all, neither pun nor sarcasm had been so very funny. The girls returned to their bread and jam. Hilary and Jennifer, like two smiling coots, moved to one side in unison, creating a space for Alison to sit down. But the humiliation was apparently not yet over.

'One moment,' came the hateful voice again. 'What d'you think you're doing now?'

'I've come to sit and have my tea.'

'Then stand up again.' A ripple of shocked embarrassment ran round the juniors. The mistress's tone had possessed a quality more vicious than they'd come to expect, even of Miss Prosser. For there had been more than a hint of menace, a tang about its delivery that shocked. This looked like a vendetta.

'Stand up again at once,' and the words fairly sizzled. 'You haven't said grace.'

It was a crude device, from a person of ill breeding. Alison knew *that* as clearly as did all the others. You could feel their general shame about the woman. But Alison was also puzzled. How could such a person come to be a mistress in any school chosen by her father? It was unthinkable and as her first introduction to authority at St Ursula's, exceedingly unfortunate. Alison was struck dumb. Though no stranger to grace, in this moment of crisis all words had deserted her.

'For what we are about to receive . . .' Hilary prompted.

'For what I am about to receive, may the Lord make me truly thankful.'

'Very well. Write out for me fifty times: "punctuality is the politeness of kings". You may sit.'

Thankful was not the word. With trembling lip, Alison sat. The mistress had resumed her tea and now Hilary gazed at the waspish form with incredulity.

'Golly,' she gasped, as the buzz of conversation began again around them, 'isn't Prosey just the most detestable heathenish bore? Fancy punishing a new girl who's five minutes late for tea?'

Alison, biting her lip, had only one observation to make. 'She doesn't like *me*. That's pretty plain.'

'Oh Daddy . . . I'm taking the opportunity to start the log as you call it, right away.'

It was later in the day, much later, on that most disastrous of all days. Had anyone in the quiet dormitory been awake, which they were not, a small ray of light might have been discerned beneath the white cover of one of the beds. Alison, by torchlight, wrote to her father: *'Beginning to write somehow makes me feel closer to you and that, above all things, is what I need just now. I don't know where you are. I'm not going to even mention it. Somehow, and I don't know how, I've just got to get through the rest of this term. Tomorrow I shall meet Miss Devine for the first time. I can't say I'm looking forward to it. But she can hardly be worse than Miss Prosser.'*

Homesickness had been just a word before. Pausing, pen to mouth, Alison slid a hand under her pillow. The gold box nestled in her hanky there, solid . . . yet as mysterious now as when she'd first spotted it. As she drew it out into the light again for a last look, a tear rolled down her cheek. But the polished surface winked a mysterious reassurance and she kissed its embossed crown, moving it softly against her lips as a charm against her enemies. Then after a quick blow on the hanky she shoved the thing back under her pillow, and settled for her first long night at St Ursula's.

CHAPTER 5

Alison Dayne always expected the worst.

It was not that on the whole she considered life treated her badly. She was not petulant or 'spoiled'. She had never flown into tempers or begged for things she was not supposed to have. On the contrary she had always been a quiet child, living inwardly and content with the smallest occupation.

With her nurse she had sat for hours in meadows, quietly plaiting grass. Her mind at that time was not occupied with thoughts that probed beyond the boundaries of the field. Indeed, she rarely asked questions. Because she took life for what it appeared to be, Alison's intellectual curiosity was fairly limited. If she saw a butterfly, she had no desire to pull it to pieces to see how it was made. She preferred to watch the curiously jerky flight and wonder at the texture of its wings.

Flowers she could name in their hundreds. But this was because she liked to extol their wild beauty later: the quality of campions clustered closely behind a woodland hedge; celandines and primroses forming a yellow carpet along the fringes of damp marshland paths. She cared little for how they functioned. As for reducing this natural world to mathematics . . . well, this was en*tire*ly beyond her scope.

Yet even amidst all that beauty, still she expected the worst . . . an animal caught in a man-laid trap for instance; so that when this worst thing happened, she would be ready for it. Yesterday she had expected the worst, and it had occurred. Now today, creeping downstairs after prayers, she was expecting it again. For this was to be the first meeting with her Head.

She had already suffered at the hands of one mistress in this school; and once bitten, twice shy. So it was without optimism that she arrived at the forbidding door. With the clear voices of the youngest children raised in song in the background, she now knocked on the panelling and listened for a stern reply.

The person who opened the door was not the Head. The face was stern all right . . . stern and sneering too. It was the face of Miss Prosser. In black mortarboard and gown, and looking like nothing quite so much as a rearing cobra, the erect figure drew back with a hiss, as if drawing in, then releasing, air.

'Ah,' she murmured, 'Alison Dayne.' Then she called: 'The Dayne girl is here Miss Devine.'

A voice bade her enter and Alison went in. She walked wonderingly through one of the most beautiful rooms she had ever seen. Palms matched its spaciousness, reminding her of one of the lazy rooms of India she had dozed in with her father. Only the slowly turning cooling fan was missing.

It had a softness that told of a comfort lacking in the girl's life just then; a sympathy that found its counterpart in the flowered cushions of the sofa, on which, spectacles balanced on the end of her nose, sat bolt upright the other newcomer of yesterday.

On another equally inviting seat sat the Headmistress, her back to the door, and Alison sensed a faint light around her head, like an aura. If only she might be nice, the girl begged silently and without hope . . . expecting, as usual, the worst. But then as she turned, this young woman with the softest and gentlest of smiles . . . a smile that was almost apologetic or rueful . . . all Alison's fear vanished away. With those placid eyes gazing for a long restorative moment into the girl's newly embittered ones, life began to ebb back.

'Welcome to St Ursula's my dear! Now why don't you come and sit by me?'

Oh, what bliss to be spoken to with courtesy . . . and what a contrast to yesterday. Coming under the maternal warmth was like sun after rain. For the first time since the death of her mother, Alison momentarily re-entered that all but forgotten state. The name in itself was enough to make you wriggle with pleasure. Miss Devine. Miss Devine . . . She could not *be* her mother for she was too young; twenty-five at the most; but of her motherliness there was no doubt.

Alison, like so many others, had fallen under a spell that was to remain with her for the whole of her life at St Ursula's. Could there be discerned some hint of a sneer in Prosser's eye, as she watched the two of them together? The pair certainly seemed to move instantly into that condition of closeness that the French call 'sympathique', but for which the English have no word.

Miss Devine spoke again. 'Maud here tells me you have already been kind to her, and that is excellent. Miss Prosser, my second mistress, on the other hand affirms that it made you late for tea. Now, you would not, I'm sure, have wished to commence your school career on the wrong foot?'

Oh . . . of course she wouldn't.

'No,' Alison declared passionately.

'Say "No Miss Devine", when you speak to your Headmistress,' Miss Prosser rapped.

'No Miss Devine,' Alison had faltered.

But it did not matter. Nothing mattered now. In the end, her father had not failed her.

'Excellent,' the Head replied. 'Maud . . .' and the magnetic regard switched to the prim figure opposite . . . 'as a scholarship girl you may find boarding school a little *different* at first. But Alison I know will always be ready with a helping hand.' She touched that hand now. There was a light firmness in the fingers that spread a glow up the girl's arm and stayed for weeks. 'I trust both your stays with us will be happy ones.'

Though no one knew then, this was a trust about to be tested, a trust that was to be tried over the ensuing weeks to the limits of one girl's endurance.

'Did you see her . . . Miss Devine I mean?'

It was Alison's first period of that first morning at school.

For Hilary there had already been one lesson to get through, and the voice that hissed penetratingly from behind the upraised desk lid was agog with anticipation.

'Yes.'

Alison looked into a pair of round eager eyes.

'Isn't she divine?'

'Silence,' came a cracking voice from the front.

27

Unfortunately it was not up to the Headmistress to provide the first taste of that other aspect of school life – the acquiring of knowledge. A doubtful privilege, it fell of course to Miss Prosser. And of all subjects, hers *had* to be mathematics.

Words have already been written about Alison's lack of science. Of her ability in maths there is less to be said. Apparently there are some people in this world who take pleasure in reducing the wonders of the natural universe to sums and equations. Alison was not of their number. Of all the subjects over which she had struggled to the despair of her governess, maths was the worst. And since her governess was none other than poor old Aunt Hester herself, very little maths had actually ever been attempted. With the book of daunting hieroglyphics spread out before her, Alison felt mounting apprehension.

The second mistress too was more than usually irritable that morning. First she had a fly in her room, waking her at half past five instead of her customary six o'clock. Then she had found in her early morning tea a disgusting half sucked boiled sweet, dropped there deliberately, she suspected, by the maid. Now she was anxious to pick on someone for her revenge. As her beady eyes roamed the class, they alighted on a most satisfactory candidate.

'Turn to page thirty-one in your Langworth and Dickinsons,' she oilily announced. 'We have two new girls in our mathematics lesson this morning . . . Maud Willison and Alison Dayne. Alison Dayne,' she purred, 'be so good as to come up here to the blackboard.'

Glory. Trapped again, Alison dragged her unwilling feet from under the desk where she sat next to the scholarship girl and plodded a path to the front.

'Kindly copy out and solve for us the algebraic problem numbered fourteen.' It was an instruction easy enough to give; easy enough indeed to copy out; less easy to solve.

Hilary whispered a few anxious words to Jennifer as they peered towards their struggling friend . . . The problem was written out, the chalk within her hand, but within her grasp the problem most certainly was not. Alison's mind had become a total blank.

I don't know whether you have ever experienced this

shaming process. If so, with all eyes upon you, you will know how unpleasant it can be. Alison felt that unpleasantness now. It was not unexpected. Much the same thing had happened the day before at tea. But it signalled a state of war.

'I'm sorry Miss Prosser,' she answered frankly. 'I can't do it.'

The mistress's mouth moved. It flattened, then it worked away in satisfaction.

Finally it curled.

'Return to your place.' The words were delivered in a sigh, that possessed all the weariness of the satisfied martyr. Miss Prosser sucked in air.

'It is disgraceful that a girl of your age should be so backward. Read and learn the whole page, and report to me before bell tomorrow morning. Maud? Show her please.'

As she rose from her seat, all eyes duly turned to Maud. The scholarship girl's brains could be seen to be fairly bursting from behind those round lensed spectacles as she stepped up to the blackboard. Sure enough, Maud easily completed the equation. Mistress and pupil exchanged fatuous smirks. It signalled a bond.

CHAPTER 6

'Gosh; wasn't Prosey hateful this morning?' Hilary pronounced with passion. The chums were sauntering up the old village street after a most exhausting first day in school. An initiation into the mysteries and rites of hockey was therefore planned for Alison that afternoon, and sticks were being shouldered along the quaint raised pavement beside thatched and timbered cottages.

'Absolutely sickening,' Jennifer agreed heartily. 'And that Maud is quite incorrigible.'

'She's a toady,' Hilary informed Alison severly. 'She seems to cling to you like an absolute leech.'

Alison agreed, for it was true.

Perhaps the budding genius from the north had simply decided to take quite literally Miss Devine's assurance about Alison's helping hand. Maud regarded her protectress from the previous night as a shining light in an otherwise fairly grey world. In spite of Alison's dimness when compared with her own oversized talent, Maud seemed to regard her companion as her personal property. But whatever else those soulful looks into Alison's nervous but not unfriendly eyes might indicate, they had not gone unnoticed by the 'twins'. Jennifer and Hilary had watched the process like hawks, and now they let rip.

'We'll have to get rid of the wet fish somehow,' Hilary declared. 'I mean . . . after all . . . she's only a scholarship creep!'

'What difference does that make?' asked Alison, puzzled.

'Well,' retorted Jennifer, as if in explanation, 'I shouldn't think her people are exactly born to the purple.'

30

Alison didn't understand this at all. A person's family was their family. Where or under what circumstances they might have been born made no difference to a girl who had lived among Indian peasants. A smarting awareness of her *own* shortcomings was what interested Alison just now.

'So what about it?' she enquired. 'Maud can do maths like some sort of machine.'

'She's got a crush on you,' Jennifer observed darkly, 'and it's going to mean trouble. Good Heavens,' she exclaimed. 'Don't look now, but she's *right* behind us.'

Indeed, trotting along with a hockey stick of her own, about twenty yards away, approached a resolute, isolated figure.

'Golly,' Hilary gasped. 'What a cheek!'

'I'll speak to her,' said Alison hastily.

'No! Run!'

The trio broke into a thundering gallop. A telephone box stood where the path to the hockey field turned away from the pavement. Inside was a man, wearing a hat and a raincoat. Staring steadily at Alison, he coolly blew a slow ring of cigarette smoke from his mouth, before turning back to the receiver.

Surely this could not be anyone she knew. And yet . . . and yet the girl had experienced an inexplicable frisson of recognition. Frowning, she turned on to the path which led to the pitch, where the groundsman could be seen marking white lines. Hilary flung the ball into the air and then clouted it with the force of a sledgehammer.

'Now you have a go,' she shouted cheerfully.

Alison obeyed. With arms flung back she attempted a mighty hit. The ball trickled forward a few feet then stopped. The girl felt a shock like an electric current running through her hands and arms.

'Sticks!' Hilary called.

'What does that mean?'

'You're not allowed to lift your stick above shoulder level,' the experts explained. Jennifer picked up the pill and replaced it carefully. 'Bully off.'

The 'twins' bent themselves to the task with deep concentration. Gasps ensued as Jennifer threw herself into the job of wrestling the ball away from Hilary.

31

'You're not doing *that* right you know,' came an admonishing Northern voice.

Red in the face, Jennifer looked up. Maud had arrived.

'Why? How d'you expect me to do it, you frabjous idiot?'

Trotting towards them across the grass, hockey stick at the ready, Maud received Jennifer's taunt unflinchingly. 'Like this.'

There was a quick clattering of sticks, then with magic ease ball and Maud together shot away down the line, past old Mr Brisling and away almost out of sight.

'Oh I say; hang on a mo, Maud,' Jennifer cried in consternation. 'How d'you come to be such a desperate ace at hockey? I didn't know they'd ever heard of the game up north?'

'Didn't you?' came a flat voice from the end of the field. 'Well you know now.'

There were suddenly two people over by the rhododendrons. Mr Brisling had been joined by a man in a raincoat and trilby hat. And now too Alison remembered where she had seen *him* . . . on the railway station and with a camera in his hands. The eyes that had bored then into hers grew larger and larger in her mind . . . till she turned and ran.

'Ali . . . where are you off to?'

'Won't be a tick,' she shouted back.

She had no thought for the consequences. She visualized only that little gold box, reposing in the place where she had that morning placed it . . . under her mattress.

It was to the school and fire escape that she ran. For Alison had already carefully noted this easy extra entrance to her dormitory, and turned to it instinctively in this moment of crisis.

The door at the top had been unlocked this morning. She hoped it would be unlocked now. She flew up the long stairway, her footsteps resounding on the metal treads, and then in at that topmost door.

In a moment she was on her knees beside her bed, her hand groping under the heavy weight of flock. The box did not seem to be there. Oh panic! Her search became frantic. Surely the ghastly man could not already have been and removed her treasure? But yes he could. That would account for his casual and blatant stare.

The possibility that he might after all have failed to recognize one particular schoolgirl amongst so many others did not even occur to her. She pushed her hand in further . . . and then, to her relief, found what she sought.

Her fingers closed round the cold smooth metal.

'What are you doing there girl?' The relief had been short lived indeed. The words rattled like hailstones. This was no male voice, and as Alison slowly looked up she confirmed that the incredible . . . the inevitable thing . . . had happened again. The words had been Miss Prosser's. The woman must be trailing her. She must be everywhere round St Ursula's at once, like a disease. Had she seen her use the fire escape? . . . that was the important point. Even Alison realized that this *must* be the crime of crimes.

But then the girl asked herself another even more unnerving question. Was Prosey too a *member of the enemy camp*? Had the woman been bribed to act as agent or spy? For a person with a background like Alison's, nothing could be ruled out. Yet surely not? No mistress in such a school could allow herself to be so misused . . . and for *money* . . . No. Not even Miss Prosser would descend to *that* Alison decided. Perhaps the mistress had always been a member of the organization? That was ridiculous too. According to Hilary, Prosey Prosser had been at this school for years and years. According to Hilary the building had been erected round her, stone by stone.

Still – after yesterday's display, anything was possible. And Alison, always expecting the worst, trusted no one. Least of all Miss Prosser.

All these thoughts rushed into Alison's mind so quickly as to be virtually simultaneous. But by the time the girl's reply came, seemingly so halting and lame, all these thoughts had been examined and her mind was made up. The woman was not going to see that box. This really *was* war now. Alison gritted her teeth. Slowly she rose to her feet.

'Oh,' she gasped, her eyelids fluttering, 'Miss Prosser . . . I thought . . .'

'Thought what?'

'Nothing,' said Alison.

'Tchk. I am not surprised.' The crabby voice was, as usual, sarcastic. Hands behind back, Alison swung to the other foot. 'Did you not know,' the mistress wearingly went on, 'that girls are forbidden to enter the dormitories during the day?'

She had *not* twigged, Alison decided with relief. She couldn't have. Why, the tone was almost reasonable!

'If you are at a loose end, go and tidy out the lost property cupboard next to the staff room. Report to me when you have finished. And Alison Dayne—' Suddenly the tone was low and menacing again. Alison felt her presence looming like a black vulture.

'Yes Miss Prosser?'

She had done the lines and taken her punishment to the gloomy study in the basement before breakfast. The page of maths was not expected to be learned till the day after tomorrow. So what could be coming?

'I do not like suspicious and furtive natures.' The mistress spoke with deadly calm. 'What do you have in your hand?'

Panic swept over Alison.

'This hand Miss Prosser?' she replied, unclenching one fist as innocently as she could.

'No. The other one.'

In agony, the second most important member of staff at St Ursula's was bobbing about like a bird, peering to see what it can find in the garden. She hoped to confirm this new girl's disobedience and unpleasantness now once and for all. There was something about this girl's face that made the blood tingle: perhaps its beauty that even the plainness of school uniform could not hide. More likely it was her infuriating air of superiority. Beneath that bland exterior the creature was laughing at *her*, Miss Prosser, in the most awful and unnerving way. The awful deduction was making the mistress's hackles rise again, just as they had risen yesterday, when Alison had first walked into tea. Slowly the second fist opened. Prosser peered. She craned. But that hand too was empty.

A school bell was ringing somewhere downstairs. For a moment the mistress hung poised between disappointment and disbelief. Then in a flurry of black cloth she turned and whirled from the room.

Alison sighed as from the confines of her sleeve the box dropped heavily into her palm. Luckily she had practised this old trick in childhood . . . and not simply for amusement either. With a father in the secret service, you never knew when such little things might come in handy. The important thing now was to act . . . before that man, or anybody else, could step out from a corridor corner to intercept . . .

The gold box had to be concealed once and for all. It must be so effectively hidden that no one would ever find it; not Prosser or anyone else. So it had to be in some secret place; somewhere undisturbed by the everyday events of school life; and the little gold object must remain there undiscovered till the end of term (or *time* if need be) . . . at least until it might be returned to its rightful owner . . . her father. Where could she hide it?

Her immediate thought was of somewhere in the woods; a cache of stones beneath tall, sympathetic trees. She had always loved the freedom of forests. Such dark, wind soughing places provided a haven for the hunted and the unloved. Alison felt vulnerable – hunted. But supposing some other much freer animal came along, dug up the trophy and carried it off to some private lair?

No, after all, the woods had better not be the place, even those darkest of tree belts that almost surrounded St Ursula's in a mysterious fringe. Better play safe. Better the grounds themselves, where she could make daily pilgrimages of inspection.

Thus her footsteps led her to the corner of the large and unprofitable vegetable garden, a place she had never seen, shut off from the world by tall sunbaked walls of mellow brick. Here were fruit trees espaliered in south facing aspects, flowers and a riot of soggy potato plants. And here too ran a sheltered conservatory, old and ornate, with moss greened glass. Under lemons and limes plant pots were ranged in profusion. Mr Brisling tended exotic seedlings as well as old geraniums; and amidst more transient blooms stood a large and permanent looking amaryllis lily. It was such a juicy white flower, on a thick stem that looked as if it had taken years to grow. Alison buried her treasure there beneath its fleshy green leaves, just deep enough in the soil to see a little gold corner . . . safe at last from prying eyes.

CHAPTER 7

'*A month has gone by* . . .' Alison wrote in her log on Saturday the eighteenth of October, '*since I saw that sinister man in the telephone box.*'

It was a kind of anniversary in a way. For though only four weeks ago it *felt* like a year since Alison had first entered St Ursula's hallowed and ancient portals.

The war with Miss Prosser persisted, simmering either just above or just below the surface according to mood.

There had been little or no contact with Miss Devine, in spite of hanging about her study door for just the occasional wistful glimpse. If it had been love at first sight, for Alison it remained love unrequited.

Rather foolishly if instinctively, for a whole week afterwards, Alison felt sure there *must* exist something more between the beautiful Headmistress and her own small self, some subtle extra force that marked her out from ordinary girls. But now this conceit had worn away. She realized ruefully there could be no favouritism, even for a motherless girl separated from her father. And in any case, Miss Prosser had gone and spoiled everything with her slimy tale telling.

The Head had been left in no doubt about Alison's standard of academic performance, as well as what Miss Prosser called 'generally unsatisfactory behaviour'. Now Alison wisely decided to shake her head and forget all about it.

Something else was increasingly puzzling the girl. Although she had nagged and nagged herself about that man, the little gold box still nestled safely in the plant pot. She began to think she'd been seeing things. Any possibility of his actually having *been* the same person as witnessed her departure by train for St

Ursula's, now seemed so remote as to be unthinkable. Until, that is, this particular deeply uninspiring Saturday afternoon . . .

The twinsome two, now firmly cemented into the triumphant three, had been hanging about since lunchtime, paralysed by the most stupid and irritating weather. A pall of fine drizzle lay over the woods and hills.

While Hilary and Jennifer lounged dispiritedly in front of the common room fire, Alison was taking the opportunity as usual to catch up with her diary:

'*Nothing at all interesting happens here Daddy*,' she was writing in gloom . . . '*unless of course you're mad about hockey. We played last week and Maud scored two goals. Next Saturday it's the great match between us and the fifth and everyone's just living for that moment. I'm not even in our team. Maud's sure to be the star. She shows me up in so many ways, yet dogs my footsteps all the time. I can't think why. She persists in viewing me as some sort of idol. I just wish she wouldn't that's all. Miss Prosser uses her to get at me. I can't stand that hateful old woman. She complains to the Head about me on the slightest pretext, always trying to humiliate me. I don't know* what's *happening to Miss Devine by the way. Lately she's been looking so awfully tired and worried. How I would like to put my arms round that slim waist and tell her comforting things . . . though not as much as I'd like to hug my dear old Dad . . .*'

At this point Alison looked up. Through the window a string of bedraggled girls could be seen, forlornly standing with hockey sticks under the dripping trees. Jennifer followed her gaze.

'The last wretched half holiday before the match,' she pronounced in a voice like a stag at bay, 'and we're *still* playing like babies!'

'You don't have to remind me,' Hilary growled into the glowing coals.

There was a sudden draught in the room. A sixth former poked her head round the door.

'Come on you three. Inspected your macs lately?'

'Our macs?' replied Hilary in a bleary voice.

'Yes. Just thought they might have been stolen.'

37

'Don't be rabid Stella,' Jennifer retorted sternly, rising from her couch and yawning. 'I saw mine there this morning.'

'Then why not give it a jolly old airing? And you can post my letter at the same time. Here. Catch.'

The missive flew across the room. As Jennifer caught it, the door closed again.

'Well . . . what a nerve. Now that madam's a prefect – she's too big for her boots altogether. *I* shan't post her beastly letter.'

'You can't very well not . . . *now*,' Hilary cackled in spite of herself, stretching luxuriously and yawning like a cat. And Alison too had felt a sudden life enter her body.

'Do let's have a walk,' she implored. 'We need some air. I've hardly seen any of the country round here.'

'No sooner said than done old sport.' Hilary flung her book across the room and bounced back into circulation.

In a moment the three had trooped down to the cloakroom and were pulling on macintoshes and wellingtons.

'Golly . . . we'll make it the grand tour,' Hilary enthused. 'I don't know why we didn't think of this before. We'll go right up past the lake . . .'

'Feeling like a *de*tour by any chance?' Jennifer enquired lightly as they squeezed arm in arm out of the back entrance. She waved the letter. 'Don't forget I've got *this* wretched thing to post. By the bye Alison . . . didn't you finish yours?'

'It wasn't a letter,' the girl dryly observed. She would never let anyone see the log; not even Hil and Jen. 'Come on,' she shouted feeling freedom in her limbs for the first time in weeks, 'let's run.'

The three burst out across the smooth lawn, recently and reverently mown by Mr Brisling. Now myriad glistening drops of water covered it as a thin film.

'Young varmints,' croaked that worthy watching them. 'Diggin' holes in my grass. They don't never think you see.'

He turned to the taller of his two companions, who sympathetically nodded. This pair were possibly the oddest ever seen at a respectable girls' boarding school and it was a good thing Miss Devine hadn't noticed them. But the old gardener was short sighted anyway and the men had money about them. It jangled encouragingly in heavy overcoat pockets. They had asked about some girl. He had answered their question and been given a shilling. Now with hockey cancelled, he was able to take his leave of the foreign gents, and stump away to toast his paws with Towser the school dog in the boiler room.

The chums were already climbing.

A stony track had left the village street, opposite the post office, slanting gently at first up through hanging beechwoods. But on the fringes of the pines above, it degenerated into a mossy path and Hilary paused to take stock of the view.

The school was clearly visible, its grounds spread out like a painting, dotted with macintoshed figures who wandered about arm in arm or were disconsolately playing tag. Between the chums and it lay an expanse of marshland, sprinkled with gates and willows and criss crossed by small streams . . .

'*That's* the straightest line up here,' Hilary explained, pointing down. 'Well not the straightest but the quickest.'

'*If* you know the way,' Jennifer laughed! 'Otherwise you're likely to get caught in a bog. Not to mention being chased by bulls.'

'Are there lots of bulls?' Alison asked, peering. 'I don't see many.'

'In the summer it's simply seething with them.'

The three turned and resumed their plodding progress.

'What Jen actually means of course is cows,' Hilary explained. 'She doesn't know the difference.'

'I do when I'm being chased,' Jennifer said solicitously.

'Well you make such funny noises! . . . flinging your arms about and squealing like you do. It's bound to make the poor souls uneasy.'

The rain had begun to patter down again, hissing into the interlacing needles above their heads, falling on to the flat, yellow-leaved bushes below. It was rain that sealed them into a world of enclosing stillness. *Still* the path snaked up, climbing through misty and seemingly impenetrable plantations. Alison said:

'Where's this lake?'

'Near the tops above Coxeley's.'

'Maybe we shouldn't go *quite* so far today?' suggested Jen.

Hilary rapped: 'Oh, Jen, *do* be quiet. Dear scrumptious ripping Miss Marriott says there are still wild pansies on the edges of those woods. I want to sleuth one down and give it to her.' The girl breathed in deeply. 'Golly! Doesn't the air feel good?'

'Mm,' Alison agreed. 'I love that smell of damp leaves.'

They stumped on hands in pockets. The forest way wound ever up into a brooding silence.

'You know,' Alison laughed, 'I think these trees are awfully spooky.' It was a good job these 'twins' knew where they going. She certainly didn't.

They had reached an overhanging hump of rock up which Jennifer scrambled till she gained the top.

'If you find the woods scary,' she yelled down after her exertion, 'just come and look up here.'

Alison followed, catching Hilary a couple of times as she slithered backward in the decaying leafy carpet. The trees were getting sparser near the top of the hill. As they emerged into the light at the stony crest, she was able to see, through the mist on the other side, an open grassy expanse with a jumble of stony walls and towers.

'Showing off our haunted castle?'

'Not *really* haunted?' Alison breathed exultantly. She loved such romantic places.

'Nobody'll go there after dark.'

'Whyever not?'

'People have seen things.'

'Ghastly shrouded figures flitting from chamber to chamber.'

Jennifer spoke with relish, Hilary visibly shivered.

'Let's go down and explore.'

'Better not Ali, actually.' Hilary spoke as if, although this was the one thing in the world she wanted to do, a sense of duty forbade it.

'Yes,' Jennifer agreed with surprising alacrity. 'It's amazing how quickly dusk gets into the woods this time of year.' They were both quite devotedly earnest, gazing at Alison with a frowning anxiety that made her want to giggle. She turned again to study the place with frowning interest. Admittedly it possessed a certain eerie dreariness, surrounded by all those dripping branches. But there was no especial reason for funk.

'Something for next time, eh?' Hilary smiled. 'Not wanting to sound feeble – but d'you think we ought to start back?'

'Aren't we going past the lakes?' Alison's disappointment burst out.

'Might, if we took the short cut?'

'Topping idea.' Hilary had brightened again. 'Then I can pick my pansy on the way.'

'D'you collect wild flowers?' Alison enquired with the curiosity of the connoisseur as they plunged straight down through the trees.

'No,' Jennifer giggled, poking her chum in the ribs. 'It really is all for Miss Marriott! She has a thing about her.'

'Well I like that,' Hilary retorted. 'Everyone in the school has. Unlike Prosey, she really makes you want to learn.' It was another excuse to wade into an ever popular topic. Soon, oblivious of their surroundings they were deep in a discussion about the merits of the various members of staff.

'Funny . . .' murmured Alison, unheard by the other two. Since this barging through tree trunks had begun to involve pushing aside creepers, and extracting oneself from ensnaring brambles, Alison felt she ought to break into what had now become quite a heated argument.

'Funny . . .' she said again loudly.

'What?'

'Funny how after a while . . .'

'Yes?'

'Well isn't it a bit strange how after a while one tree begins to look like another?'

'Does it?'

The twinsome pair stopped arguing and looked about them. Trees pressed closely on all sides.

'Don't worry.'

Jennifer spoke confidently. She was anxious to get back to Miss Patterson who had only yesterday given her two sweets, and not the ordinary kind either. They were the ones with the buttery stuff inside that really squirted down your chin, the ones that Jennifer would herself have chosen, had she had the ready cash at the right time and in the right place. 'Worry not, mon vieux chou,' she advised. 'We can't be all that far away now.'

'Yes,' Hilary agreed. 'We'll soon see a gleam of water . . . though I must say,' she added, frowning, 'it'll soon be too dark to see *anything* much.'

They climbed up a little hillock. It was supposed to be a viewpoint, but all they could see was a moist sea of feathery firs.

'Is this the way *actually* Jen?' There was a stern note to Hilary's voice.

'Don't ask me,' Jennifer grumbled. 'You were the one who wanted the lake.'

'I wasn't.'

'You were.'

'I wasn't. I don't even like lakes; and if you're trying to say something else, I should spit it out . . .'

'All right,' came the plonking reply. 'We're lost.'

Flummoxed at last, the 'twins' looked about them.

'So what do we do now?'

'At least the rain's stopped,' Alison observed helpfully.

Hilary sank back against a tree.

'Hang it all Jen. It's not my fault.'

'Nobody said it was . . .'

'You did. You just said that very thing – or a minute ago anyway. You said . . .'

'Hang on a mo,' Alison interrupted, her head twisted to one side and listening, 'but isn't that the sound of a car?'

There was a general straining of ears. Then Hilary leapt into the air.

'Goodness,' she yelped. 'The girl's a marvel. There must be a road down there,' she was carolling as they leapt over boulder and crag, careering through the trees and yelling 'Stop! Stop!' as if their lives depended on it . . . which if Alison's experiences were anything to go by, in a way they did.

And in a very few moments they had burst out on to a road. It was really little more than a track through the trees, a winding forest lane that got lost in the mist just a little way ahead. But *there* was that throbbing sound again, and as a vision of Miss Prosser waiting for them as they slunk in late rose like a spectre in the grey sky, the girls wrung their hands in desperation.

'It hasn't *gone* has it? . . . gone by already I mean?'

It hadn't. At that moment the blunt brass nose of a long green open tourer erupted round a bend and was travellng towards them at a slow bumping pace, as though feeling its way through hostile enemy territory.

What would a car be doing along here anyway, Alison was asking herself as Jennifer flung herself into the road and began to wave her arms wildly. There was no time to answer. The vehicle was upon them. With a thump of brakes badly manipulated, it jerked to a halt.

'Yes . . . who are you? What do you want?'

The staccato question had come from an unusual man. Indeed a more unexpected pair would be difficult to imagine down an English country lane. 'Blooming foreigners' Mr Brisling had called them . . . 'more like Count Dracula.'

It had been the one in the passenger seat who had spoken, a giant with a hook nose. His black eyes flashed beneath a hat of matching astrakan while the stolid peak capped chauffeur beside him glowered straight ahead into the fog.

'I say,' Jennifer was already gasping, 'we're fearfully sorry, but could you give us a lift?'

'Here . . . hang on a mo Jen . . .'

Hilary, who had decided she didn't awfully like what she saw, felt a sudden qualm. 'D'you think we ought?'

'Shut up Hil.'

Jennifer's only concern at that moment was to be back in school and safely installed at the tea table. 'We're a bit lost you see, and it's getting rather late.'

'But certainly my dear child.' The cruel mouth twisted instantly into a roguish smile, the grey bearded face alive suddenly with rare humour. He looked from one to the other of them, his eyes searching their faces with hawkish intensity. 'We shall be only too pleased to take you wherever you want to go.'

The accent had a mid-European lilt, and, like the face, was for some inexplicable reason disturbingly familiar to Alison.

'St Ursula's you know; our school,' Jennifer prattled on. But Alison had clicked.

It was too late. The man had already swung over his seat to open the back door of the car and was now commanding:

'Get in . . . all of you please.'

Under the power of a penetrating frown, Alison felt her

valuable life blood beginning to ebb away. There was no time to back out now. Indeed Jennifer had already climbed in and Hilary was grumpily following. Stuffed between them in the rear seat, Alison's only way was to affect complete indifference. How she blessed the anonymity of her navy blue mac, and what a blessing to have a hat to pull over your face.

'Do you not realize,' her father would have said, and she could just hear his voice . . . 'that that's what uniform is *for*?'

All right for him, she thought bitterly. A secret service officer was presumably trained for just such situations as this. She on the other hand was not and she prayed that her fears were unfounded; that it had been a chance meeting; that the men were after all perfectly innocent members of the English travelling public . . . on their way to visit a grave in some local haunted castle. It had been four weeks since the incident beside the village telephone box. These characters were flamboyant enough to have just stepped off the Orient Express and if they were agents for some foreign power, why had they waited so long?

Perhaps that was just it. Perhaps the other lot had been mere minions, spies sent out to prime the ground for the arrival of their superior. He might be the head of the Secret Police. For there was a cocky arrogance about this person who sat with his back to them in the front seat. In massive grey topcoat and collar of black curled fur, his cheerful tones struck a knell of doom.

'As a matter of fact,' he was now announcing, 'this is all most opportune, since we ourselves are searching for that very school.'

Yes, of course, they would be doing that. With all doubt now removed, Alison pulled down her hat even further over her face. She simmered in mounting fury. The cheek of it. The actual confounded cheek of thinking . . . no . . . of *knowing* they could catch her out in such an obvious manner. Oh, how stupid she'd been not to realize immediately who they must be. Now the creature was talking again, this time to his companion.

'What did you say the name was?'

'St Ursula's,' growled the chauffeur in a queer Scottish voice. 'St Ursula's . . . yes of course. Excellent. Excellent.'

The man's patronising joviality was galling beyond belief. Rebellion had set in again. Alison had not the faintest idea of what might happen, but she could be as sullen and uncooperative as a donkey when the need arose – as Miss Prosser had already discovered to her cost. The man grinned round villainously.

'Comfortable I trust?'

'Yes thank you.' Jennifer was feeling in the gayest of moods. 'Why,' she asked blandly, 'do you want to go to our school?'

'It is interesting you should ask that question. The Major here . . .'

'*Major*?'

'. . . the Major knows very well the father of one of your girls.' Hilary sat up, while Alison sagged down.

'Really?'

Unnoticed, the foreigner had slid his hand under his topcoat and from his pocket produced an enlarged photograph. With Alison's features framed in the driving mirror, he compared them with those in the enlargement and his voice then lifted in crisp satisfaction:

'They were together at the war office,' he shouted above the noise of the engine, 'before being for a short time on a . . . how do you call it, Major?'

'Mission,' supplied the chauffeur, sourly twisting his nose, 'a secret mission.'

The photograph was quietly replaced.

'Golly.'

How easily Jennifer was impressed, Alison sighed bitterly. She could not be blamed. Secret missions; secret agents; such things entered but rarely, one assumed, into school life.

'Exciting isn't it? We have a message from him.'

'Oh? What was his name?' Hilary enquired.

'Dayne. A Colonel Dayne.'

Had the car been motionless, you might have heard a pin drop.

'But that's ridiculous!' Jennifer burst out at last. Alison sank even lower.

'Why so ridiculous?'

'Ow!' Of a less dim nature altogether, Hilary had dug her friend in the ribs.

'Oh . . . no reason,' Jennifer hastily assured them.

'Naturally,' came the smooth voice again, 'the communication being of a confidential nature, we would wish to speak to his daughter in private.'

The car had now turned into, and was rumbling along, the school drive. A silence of consternation reigned between all three in the back seat. Between Alison and these most curious of foreigners, something fishy was going on. But however pleasant on occasion it might be to poke into other peoples' affairs, this was evidently for Hil and Jen neither the time nor the place.

Smoothly the car turned in front of the old grey building until it faced in the opposite direction, ready no doubt for a quick getaway, should the need arise. It did not arise. Darkness had almost fallen. There was no one about.

'Oh, gosh yes.' Jennifer spoke hastily, as if after a long absence. 'Thanks most awfully for the lift. Come on Hil.'

'You coming Ali?' Hilary spoke timidly to the daughter of Colonel Dayne, with whom these people wished to speak in private.

'No, it's all right Hil. You go.'

And they went. Having climbed from the car, they left as fast as their legs would carry them. For Alison there was no such option. She had to see this thing out. 'Yes,' she gritted. 'I'm Alison Dayne.'

The hook nosed man turned. With an ever widening smile he raised his upturned palms.

'What an amazing coincidence,' he said wonderingly. 'You recognize the likeness, Brigadier? . . . I mean Colonel?'

'I most certainly do.'

Get on with it, Alison growled to herself. 'What is the message?' she snapped.

'Oh . . . the message is quite simple. Your father tells us that when you were on your way to school and at the railway station, he gave you something to keep for him . . . but which he would now like you to give to me.'

'What did he give me to keep?' Alison persisted doggedly, but fear was taking hold of her. Why did the other two have to scoot off so quickly? The girl felt on the edge of an abyss, as she had in childhood nightmares. Everyone in the school seemed to be watching. Surely they must all be watching her from behind those black windows? But no one stepped forward.

'A little . . . a little bag was it not, Major?' The foreigner's

46

eyes, like a lizard's tongue, were darting all over her face. The chauffeur replied with just a suggestion of a smile . . .

'Something like that.'

'I have no little bag.'

'My dear child,' snapped the voice, suddenly honing to razor sharpness, 'I think you have.' A snaking hand suddenly had her wrist in a grip of steel. The man was breathing heavily into her face and Alison recoiled sharply.

'Alison?' Like a light in a storm Miss Devine's voice came from somewhere behind.

The grip and manner slowly relaxed. Through sullen disappointment the man forced a smile. The harsh voice laughed.

'Naturally I might have known such a daughter of an English gentleman would not be taken in so easily. We were *testing* you and you have emerged with the flying colours. Maybe, Miss Dayne, you would be willing to help at another time? . . . if you have some proof of our identity? Possibly a letter from your father, eh? Be here in exactly one week's time, and you shall have it.'

A hand of friendship was stuck out but Alison sprang from the car. The Headmistress was visible in the porch. She had not come any further – perhaps because of the rain.

Alison strode quivering towards her rescuer. The by now quite jovial voice was calling: 'Your father sends you his best wishes.' With a scrunch the car drove off. Alison broke into a run. She was back. She was being received back from a hostile real world into a protective encircling arm.

The Head led Alison into the school, and searching her face said, 'Who were those people you were with in the car?'

Alison shivered, the voice sounded so strained.

'I don't know Miss Devine. There was a foreign sounding man and a Scots chauffeur . . . a Major someone. We were late and they gave us a lift.'

'Good *Heavens* child! Do you not realize you must never on any account accept lifts from strangers? Now Alison, come along inside. I want to talk to you alone.'

They stepped together into the cosy fire lit confines of Miss Devine's study. The Headmistress crossed over to the windows and with a sharp definitive gesture closed the curtains. Not until all traces of the outside had been shut away did she appear to feel it safe to speak.

'Now.' The young woman turned and gazed poignantly at her charge. 'What did this "foreign sounding" gentleman say?'

Alison shifted uneasily. Moving from one wellington boot to the other, she clasped hands and knit her brow.

'He pretended to know my father.'

'You mean,' Miss Devine interrupted incredulously, 'you told him your name?'

Alison looked up.

'He knew it already,' she replied, dolefully.

Alison found herself propelled by a firm hand towards the fire. The two sat down together. In the most anxious of voices, the Head asked urgently, 'He asked *questions* about your father?'

At least on one point Alison was able to reassure the tense, birdlike figure and she shook her head vigorously.

'Oh *no*. I told him nothing.' There was a pause. Lifting eyes to the Headmistress's face, the girl admitted: 'Oh Miss Devine . . . I'm frightened.'

The Head subsided. In yielding warmth, all severity crumbled. 'There is no need to be, child.'

Ruefully smiling, Miss Devine took the smaller colder hand in her own and began to squeeze it tight . . . 'What safer place can exist than a school such as ours?' Looking down, Alison felt the heat flowing from that real and infinitely reassuring pressure and her chest collapsed in a long exhalation. A log fell. The room was quiet and still. As she gazed into its cosiness a glow spread through all her limbs and through herself . . . until the tension she had not really even been aware of ebbed away . . . and at last vanished. It was almost absently, and without taking away her hand that the Head then turned away – to ask:

'One other quite incidental thing . . . Did this man at any stage mention . . . me? Or a person called Stephen?'

'No Miss Devine, he did not.' The girl shook her head. Her heart began to beat faster again. 'Did you expect him to?'

There could be no doubt of the Head's agitation. Frowning intensely, she suddenly burst out: 'I am distracted, Alison.

Stephen is my little brother. He and I have known this man in the past . . . unhappily.'

Suddenly she seemed to have taken a plunge as though she had decided that, after all, Alison was not so very much younger than herself and so she could speak frankly to her. Turning a tragic face she stammered: 'Now Stephen has disappeared.'

'Disappeared?'

Gulping, Alison desperately tried to comprehend what had been quite obviously a cry from the heart. Why the Head-mistress had taken it on herself to confide in a mere schoolgirl was too much at that moment for her to understand, but as she heard the answer: 'Yes; from school; I heard the news today . . .' Alison knew this to be the most important moment of her life, as if she had suddenly graduated . . . into being a grown up person.

'Why are you telling *me*?'

'Because,' the Head told her distractedly, 'because I can't help feeling that between you and me, Alison my dear, there exists . . .' Miss Devine was evidently struggling for words . . . 'a certain affinity . . . a certain bond.'

Having actually committed herself, Miss Devine looked up dumbly. Was she shivering?

'Oh no,' the mistress declared . . . 'that is ridiculous of course.' She laughed; almost hysterically. 'I should never have men-tioned it. The fact is, there has been no one else to talk to and I thought that you, being for the moment fatherless and quite alone yourself . . . might understand.' The Head bit her soft red lip and raised her eyebrows in question. To a detached observer it might have seemed a rather hopeless, even ridiculous situation.

'Oh,' the girl sighed fervently . . . 'if only I could.'

The stupid thing was that she *did* understand of course. For a long moment the two gazed penetratingly at each other.

Many strange questions danced in the air between them. Was the Head also trying to summon the courage to say something *else*? Or were these halting phrases some probe, an attempt to discover the extent of Alison's own knowledge of a riddle that seemed suddenly to have come between them? Poor

Alison. Caught in such a tangle, she could hardly formulate the questions, let alone the answers. Even to confide in her own Headmistress was not a decision that could be taken lightly. She knew the rules of her father's game better, sometimes, than he did himself. Discretion had become second nature over the years. It was a habit hard to break. To the 'twins' of course, finding a little gold toy in the centre of a box of chocolates had seemed less important than the chocolates themselves. Family jokes . . . even such eccentricities as this had to be respected. Most grown ups were mad anyway; especially one's own relations. So of course the two had tactfully let the matter drop. There is, after all, a code, among honourable English schoolgirls.

'*With the Head*,' Alison gloomed over her diary dated October 26th, '*things ought to have been different. I suppose I should have told her.*'

But then, as on that fateful following Saturday afternoon, her thoughts went winging back to Miss Devine's final cryptic admission. Alison cringed.

'It's foolish of me to behave like this,' the young woman had gasped. 'Say nothing to the other girls.'

Oh, it had been so awful somehow. Of *course* Alison would say nothing. Whether now, seven days later, Stephen had been found, she had not had the slightest hint. But exactly one week had passed since the painful scene . . . and the girl had that *other* worry haunting her. At three this very afternoon two men were supposed to be bringing her a message. This was a dilemma from which there could be *no* escape. And, however much wiser it might have been to do so, Alison turned again, not to Miss Devine, but to her father.

'*Daddy*,' she agonized to her diary, '*I'm in such a quandary. In an hour I'm supposed to meet those men. If I go and they don't have anything from you at all . . . which I'm sure they won't . . . they could attack and overpower me. Then I might blurt out about your treasure. But if you* have *actually given them a letter and I stay away, well, such beastliness doesn't bear thinking about. It's the great game today. I should have so loved to just go and watch Maud run rings round the fifth . . . without a care in the world. Now I'm totally stymied. Oh . . . if only someone would come in and simply tell me what to do . . .'*

At that moment the common room door crashed open and a heavily breathing Hilary appeared, framed in the entrance.

'Alison,' she panted, 'you've got to come and get ready. Maud's pulled a muscle in her leg. You're playing in the match.'

CHAPTER 8

'Oh, well done Fiona . . . pitch it strong.'

The hockey was progressing vigorously and the clear voices of fifth formers rang out along a packed touch line.

'Tatiana. Look where you're going!'

'Give it 'em hot Esme. We're behind you.'

And then in more squeaking tones:

'Hurrah for the fourth. There'll be feasting tonight.'

In fact this latter observation was made more in desperation than in hope since the early successes of the younger girls had now been reversed and the score stood at two goals all. With the final minutes of the second half ticking away, the result seemed inevitable at last.

But this was nothing if not a battle to the death. Goaded by the aloofness of their hated rivals, the fourth formers put every ounce of energy into the game. Flinging themselves so much about the pitch, they quite often found they were tripping up even their own side and then sliding long distances in the mud. But what the fourteen year olds lacked in size and experience, they made up in furious determination; and even now Tryphena Hargreaves had wrested the ball from a great big sulky girl in mid-field and was breaking away at last to race well past the three-quarter line. The juniors screamed their excitement . . .

'Searching for the tragic muse Lois? You'll need it the way things are going . . .'

'I say, that's pretty fair cheek . . . oh . . . sportsman Enid.'

Impudent imp put down, the said Lois could breathe again with the rest of her clan. For once again those solid impenetrable backs had foiled a noble attempt at goal. Now they'd got wise to all the fourth's little tricks, and for Maud who had so carefully planned the whole thing it was a period of intense frustration.

Academic brilliance did little for a person's image at St Ursula's . . . rather the reverse. Success on the hockey field however was quite a different matter and Maud had put all her faith in this match. Through it, the scholarship girl had hoped to be at last accepted at St Ursula's, not as an intellectual marvel of science but simply one of the crowd.

She wanted to melt easily into those mysteries of behaviour that seemed to be taken for granted by the rest of them . . . as Alison had done, without apparently even trying. What Maud would have given for Alison's two natural advantages . . . breeding and good looks. At times she'd even envied the girl's dimness in class and would willingly have accepted Miss Prosser's scourging sarcasms in her place. She could have taken with impunity such blows as were aimed at her beloved champion, for life can be hard in the north of England. Acutely aware of her loneliness and frustration, Alison for her part had continued to sit next to the other new girl through those endless baffling trials of Latin and mathematics. And curiously, if Maud suffered, she still suffered too.

But the crowd can be heartless. Alison, though alone in her soul, had been as naturally accepted in the school as a pea in a pod. Not so Maud; to be one of the crowd, that was the poor thing's only aim. And now, with that stupid fall just before the match, all her hopes had been dashed. Right there two minutes before the starting whistle it had happened, and as a sop they made her umpire. It was not much of a consolation, but at least they had let Alison play in her stead.

Oh how Maud tried to give the other girl her mental strength, her facility for concentration, willing her to succeed. But if there was any temptation to ignore any little fouls that might interfere with her heroine's success, it was temptation resisted. Maud was nothing if not thorough and she had eyes like a hawk. *All* fouls were checked at source. In the crowd there had already been rumblings of complaint about it. And quite a lot of the muttering re this excessive zeal came from the sixth. They were not *all* too high and mighty to watch the endeavours of their inferiors. With two school teams to fill,

53

they came to watch for talent and they hated anything that slowed the game down. In an internal battle where tempers ran high, it was best not to meddle overmuch. Better they fought it out on the games field than afterwards in the pavilion.

Maud, preoccupied in willing her friend to greater and greater efforts, failed to notice the mounting hostility that was to be her downfall. Oh, it was the last thing she would have wanted or even understood, for in that willing and anxious heart lay the streak of basic honesty and fair play that characterizes an indomitable northern spirit.

Unfortunately, the northern spirit is something quite alien to smooth and supple limbed angels in the south. It was one of *these* girls that now shouted out in lofty and languid tone, her voice vibrating effortlessly through the throng: 'Give the wretched whistle a miss Maud . . .' just as Alison, in possession at last, was dodging with the ball rather haphazardly down the wing. The command had come from none other than the Head Girl herself. Paralysed; realizing at this late moment her incipient unpopularity, Maud had faltered. Even those stalwart backs had relaxed their guard after that imperious cry. And so it was that Alison, having dredged her way along the line without too much opposition, suddenly found herself right in the semicircle in front of her opponents' goal.

It was as much of a surprise to Alison as to everyone else. But then came something even more unnerving. For even as she paused to consider her next move, from over the top of the bushes ahead there appeared two anxious faces. They were unmistakable.

Alison's eyes remained for a moment riveted and her limbs paralysed. Having evidently caught sight of her, the bearded giant had produced a piece of paper and grinning now, waved and tapped it encouragingly.

'Come on Ali . . . Shoot.'

Automatically her stick lifted high, high. Then as wood and leather met with a satisfying thunk, the ball sped unerringly into the net.

'Goal!'

No one else had noticed the weird gesticulating figure. With their attention firmly in the goalmouth, pandemonium broke out amongst the crowd.

'Sticks! Hurrah! Foul! Cheers! Hurrah! Sticks!'

'Goal!'

Maud's whistle had shrilled. She was signalling a goal, there could be no doubt about it. The fifth were incredulous! For Alison's stick had risen palpably and for all to see at least two whole feet above her shoulder, an unmistakable and inescapable foul.

'Sticks. It *was* sticks you fathead.'

Ten minutes earlier, Maud would have agreed in the best interests of the game. Now her blood was up. Her temper rose. All her repressed resentment threatened to boil over. Their arrogant retorts cut to the quick of her rapidly beating heart. They were simply *not fair*. Somehow, incredibly, they seemed to think they could have it both ways. All that stuff about honour and fair play . . . they were snobs, the lot of them. Be hanged to their protests. Maud dug in her heels. And when Maud dug in her heels they usually stayed fairly entrenched.

'If I say it was a goal,' she yelped, with now not the least attempt to moderate her accent, 'then it *was* a goal. I'm the umpire, and the umpire's decision is final.'

Alison, the cause of the row, was not even listening. Instead she was gaping bleakly at a clump of bushes. Should she quickly run there now, just to check? She could hardly be kidnapped, in full view of everyone. But even as she craned to see, she spotted their low scurrying figures, waving and gesticulating for her to follow as they skulked to another cover.

'Sillyass,' someone was shouting from the touch line. 'Just because Alison's your wretched dream girl . . .'

'Yes . . . if it had been anyone but *darling* Alison . . .'

Alison stood torn. If these men really *had* important information, be assured they would seek her out as inexorably as ferrets. And now, as Maud's turn came to swing furiously towards her 'idol', the heads bobbed out of sight. This clinched it. No friend of her father would behave in such a ludicrous manner. Alison turned. She had made her decision and ran back over to the crowd.

'Alison?' Maud was pleading. 'What do *you* say?'

The girl drew in her breath for an honest reply that had to come.

'It *was* sticks Maud. I'm always doing it.'

Knowing the effect it would have, the confession made her squirm, but how could she have said anything else?

'Above all . . . never, never tell a lie . . .'

Disbelievingly the scholarship girl gaped. Then her eyes narrowed.

'Right,' she snapped. Without another word she turned and limped from the field.

Unnerved and rueful, Alison gazed after the pathetic and worrying figure. Had the game not had to progress to its weary conclusion, she would have run after her . . . but there were still five minutes left.

'Golly, she's cracked,' rang out one clear voice after another as they returned to their places. 'A regular duffer. Totally unsporting.'

'What can you expect from one of *those*?'

'Still . . . jolly sporting of Alison to concede like that.'

Alison had no particular desire to be 'sporting' as they called it. The word at that moment irritated her, as much as it would have irritated Maud. If only these girls wouldn't *gush* so. She had told the truth – already she was regretting it. *Whatever* she did seemed to be wrong, that was all Alison knew at this moment. The dozing Miss Sanders had been roused in her lair by cries from the seniors of:

'Umpire! New umpire!'

Now the sports mistress ran out on to the field shouting irritably, 'All right girls . . . penalty bully.'

And that was virtually the ignominious end of an extremely disheartening game.

As they poured back into the pavilion, ten of the eleven foreheads were creased in frustration.

'A draw. Rotten luck *I* call it. Absolutely sickening. No excuse for a dormy feast after all.'

Hilary swung on the speaker with a swift rebuttal. 'Stow it Tryphena. We didn't lose did we?'

'No; but we'd have won if Alison hadn't . . .'

'Yes? If Alison hadn't . . . ?'

'Here I say! What's this you beasts?'

'Sit on her.' They moved in threateningly.

'What you said was just a mean bit of nastiness Tryphena. Scrag her someone.'

They sat and they scragged. Alison could only watch. She peered in bewilderment. The support was all for *her*. As Tryphena bumped to the hard wooden floor, it was difficult to hear a word for the defence. It was difficult to hear because there were five healthy young bottoms sitting on Tryphena's face. Eventually a strangled voice emerged, muffled by gym slips.

'Pax! Oh my hat! I didn't mean anything. We'll have the feast anyway. Alison's wonderful. Ask anyone in the school . . .'

A steady blush rose to the roots of Alison's hair. She hated being singled out. But Hilary was grinning at her like the giddy goose, and slipping an affectionate arm through hers whilst affirming:

'You as *good* as won it for us, eh old thing? We'll show our appreciation tonight, never fear.'

'Oh gosh yes.' Here was Jennifer taking the other arm and giving it a hearty squeeze. 'I simply can't wait for nine o'clock.'

If you belong to the band of critics who think the tradition of dormy feasts infantile nonsense, you would not have received much support at St Ursula's. For St Ursula's was addicted to this unhealthy form of feeding. The ritual mesmerized young and old alike, whether hungry or not.

There was a terror attached to its sin, a glamour about the danger of discovery that no one had ever been able to eradicate. For years Miss Prosser had been trying to do just that. It was back in the mists of time that she'd declared war on the hallowed institution. But since the awareness of her hovering nearness lent such a deadly fascination to the whole thrilling business, she was unlikely ever to succeed in stamping out such acts of 'flagrant disobedience'. Let us face the fact. Prosser too had had plenty of time to become a tradition at St Ursula's. She had been at the school for as long as anyone could remember, or as some of the tinies agreed in horrified tones . . . for ever. Perhaps, once, she had been a slip of a girl herself. All the indications were that she had not. Even at this very moment as the juniors were settling themselves down for the night in their own particular way, they knew that, true to form, the mistress would be hovering . . . Some said she had no shadow.

Be that as it may, twittering like a bat, Prosser flitted. Tirelessly darting, hither and thither, hoping to hear some revelry she might expunge, the mistress clung to the ancient walls, and rustled down the passages.

Quite unwilling to dare trust the prefects to switch off the dormitory lights themselves, she would hang about draughty corners like a tormented, restless ghost. Not for Miss Prosser the quiet satisfaction of a good dinner taken with wine at a civilized hour. Sufficient for her sinewy frame were the thin slices of bread and butter taken at tea, with perhaps an isosceles triangle of plum cake or a square of madeira, and cold rice pudding to finish. Not that she liked rice pudding. Indeed she had an aversion to the sticky delicacy. But she always took it when offered, for this distaste represented a flaw in her makeup, and was one she was determined to conquer.

Imagine then her disquiet when, on her way specifically to Nightingale to put down those most disobedient of all fourth formers . . . she was arrested by a plump and finger licking Miss Marriott with a rice pudding to share. Miss Prosser had forgotten she had made this arrangement with the botany mistress for a mutual perusal of new books for the library, books she privately considered incipiently dangerous to young minds and which had much better be destroyed. And thus it had fallen to Marjorie Mearcroft to shine her torch round a dormitory of unnaturally quiet junior girls.

Yet peacefully as most of them lay, flat out in their little white beds, there was still one bed where all was *not* well. From the place next to Alison came the signs of upheaval. It sounded like snivels, and yet the girls felt little sympathy for the sniveller. The prefect shone her torch. A white strained face gazed pathetically up into the cold and merciless beam. It was a face that streamed with tears, and an embarrassment to everyone.

'What's the matter with *her*?' the older girl enquired wearily.

'She's upset about the match.'

'Oh? She was the umpire wasn't she? Pretty bad form

58

running off like that.'

'I should ignore her. She's only shamming.'

The monitress clicked her tongue. 'Is something wrong?' she enquired.

It was a pity in a way that it had *not* been Miss Prosser, for Maud was the one girl in the school with whom the tyrant mistress might have sympathized.

'No, no, no,' came the reply of truculent insistence. A set of healthy teeth ground deeply into an inoffensive school pillow. It was a pillow that at this troubled time offered little comfort. The blood of its owner had been deeply stirred and all the obstinacy of the Willisons was evident in that retort.

'Then might I ask you in the nicest possible way to pipe down?'

'Oh buzz off,' Maud replied succinctly . . . 'you and all the rest of your stuck up cronies. You're all the same . . . ghastly.'

'Maud Willison.' The tone of the prefect showed how deeply she had been shocked. 'When will you learn that monitresses have some authority around here?' There was a pregnant pause. 'Lose two order marks.' The older girl flicked her torch round the others. 'Now go to sleep . . . all of you.'

The light was switched off. The door closed. The footsteps were heard pattering off down the corridor and for a full minute silence reigned. Then six pairs of legs swung from beds.

'Got the torch you fourth form feasters?'

'Yes, here it is. Come on. Wheel out the grub . . .'

As the lid of the big tuck box swung open an ecstatic and unstinting admiration of its contents was already thrilling out, in just those extravagant phrases Maud detested so much.

'Oh . . . ripping; gorgeous; wonderful grub. What's your cream doughnut like Philippa? Mine's simply divine.'

There was cake: cherry cake, chocolate cake, plum cake. There were doughnuts and cream horns, brandy snaps, meringues and eclairs in a profusion that would have confused a starving man. They had been sent by parents anxious only that their offspring should have enough to eat and very little concerned for the sylph like figures of their daughters. At home these girls lived on the fat of the land. To Maud this was disgustingly obvious. She loathed them all, she was thinking, as Alison crossed over to her bed, her head downcast and apologetic.

'Maud – I'm sorry about this afternoon. I didn't want to show you up or anything.'

'You're not sorry,' Maud retorted. 'You're just like all the rest – all so cocksure with your la-di-da voices.'

'Come on Ali,' Hilary called. 'The cake's getting stale.'

'I don't like your sort Alison Dayne,' Maud wrenched out . . . 'you're a toad. In fact I hate you.'

It was a total reversal of feelings and one which she must have realized she would regret later. But there was no backing down. If Maud had wanted to sting her beloved into some sort of reaction, she succeeded.

'Don't *say* things like that.' Alison felt truly shocked, and as much for Maud's sake as her own. Nobody had ever said they hated her before. The experience was not pleasant.

'Hate's a nasty word Maud,' Jennifer warned amidst a shocked silence.

Having at last captured the stage, Maud was disinclined to yield. Some little devil inside her made her press home an advantage born from long practice. Quite probably her mother, that lady in the northern sweet shop, had also had a taste of such moods.

'It's true,' Maud flared. 'She thinks if she carries on creeping up to Miss Devine the way she has been doing, she'll never get into trouble again.' The words came so easily even Alison stopped and blinked.

It was true that since the thrill of that last meeting there *had* been a curiously expanding awareness between pupil and mistress. Now it seemed Maud too was aware of a liaison that she jealously regarded as a threat.

'You're a *toady* Alison Dayne,' she was crying out, sobbing the words that had already begun to stick in her throat. 'Do you hear?' The girl *knew* she had gone just a step too far.

'I am not a toady.'

'All right,' came the reckless reply. 'So prove it.' Jaws suspended, the feasters gaped . . . 'Let's see you do something *really* bad for a change.'

Now at last Jennifer found her voice.

'These are strong words Maud,' she gasped, 'even for you.'

'Oh are they really?' Maud's imitation of the southern accent was both bitter and biting. 'Shut your mouth snob face. I want to see what Miss Dayne's really made of.'

'Don't talk nonsense . . . please Maud,' Alison pleaded.

But there was no halting the flow. The injured umpire had slipped into gear. With that reckless habit of throwing caution to the wind that is supposed to characterize northern arguers the girl now retorted:

'Nonsense? I'm not talking nonsense you po faced jellyfish. I'm issuing a challenge. Nonsense! she says in that high falutin' voice . . .'

Certainly Maud did *not* know when to stop. The challenge came as a pique to the honour of the whole dormitory and was one they could not ignore.

'You mean . . . a *dare*?' Hilary, as unspoken leader, responded instantly and hotly.

'I mean exactly that. Alison Dayne . . . I dare you to go now to . . . yes, to that old haunted castle place, and bring something back to prove to everyone here that you actually went . . .'

'But that's absurd,' Alison argued. To Alison it was perhaps absurd . . . but not to Jennifer. Maud's judgement of her school fellows had been shrewd. For Jennifer, with the good name of the dorm at stake and Alison wavering, there seemed only one thing possible, and that was to accept the challenge on her friend's behalf.

'You needn't ask for proof you silly worm,' she snapped back. 'Our word'll be good enough. Are you for it Hil?'

'Absolutely. I'm game if you are.'

'As game as can be.'

'Just a minute . . .' Alison had found her voice.

'Yes old thing?'

'Well what about me?' she hooted. 'Maud's challenge was to me. Where do *I* fit in?'

'*Right* in old inseparable. You're the leader of the jolly little party.'

'But I don't want to go,' Alison wailed. 'It's cold and I'm tired. I've never heard a more stupid idea.'

To Maud's satisfaction, the response to this perfectly

61

reasonable objection was characteristically short.

'You *are* joking of course. No one can refuse an actual dare.'

'Unless,' added Maud in triumph, 'that person's a toadying little creep, who's frightened she might get caught.'

Of couse that clinched the matter. Maud had played her cards only too well – the challenge could not be avoided; even Alison realized it at last. Just wait till they got back, that was all, then someone'd get a piece of somebody's mind.

It was the work of a moment to slip on dressing gowns and shoes. Alison pocketed her trusty torch. They opened the door and then, watched by four pairs of rounded, goggling eyes, crept down the fire escape. For the anxious watchers left behind, the dormy feast had taken on a new meaning. Its wickedness had entered an altogether different league for now there was really something to celebrate – a daredevil escapade that rivalled any in fiction. They were spies – criminals – all of them, including Maud, awaiting the return of their comrades from a mission as dangerous as anything from a newspaper.

Several minutes elapsed. If Prosser had been alerted she would have been up by now. With any luck she'd be marking exercise books, inscribing neatly with red ink 'this is wrong', and giving two out of ten to Alison Dayne for her geometry. But if she *did* suddenly squeeze her head round the door, however, they would need a contingency plan. Maud settled back with a quiet smile of repose into the warm comfort of her bed as, with lowered voices, the others discussed just what they'd do if such a frantic situation arose.

Outside meanwhile, at least two stalwart sleuths had been gripped by the thrill of the mission.

'Isn't this a lark?' Jennifer carolled, throwing up her hands and doing a cartwheel over the damp grass. 'We hardly need the torch, the moon's so bright.'

Huge and silvery, the great orb rode through the clear heavens. Its light spread like silver paint over the glossy leaves. The path ahead was lit by an unearthly glow that had filtered through the branches of trees and lay as a languid dappled web. Whatever else it might have illumintated it failed to brighten Alison's disconsolate face, however.

'What's up Ali? You're not saying much.' Jennifer sobered

down enough to peer anxiously at her friend. Too many times already this term, Alison had crossed Miss Prosser's path. One more might be just one time too many . . . and what would happen to Alison then? If she were to be expelled from this school, there was nowhere else to go. There would be nobody at home; nobody to look after her at all. With no means of contact, she would not even be able to tell her father. Expulsion . . . yes that had to be the worst. With so many other more important issues at stake, Alison could have done without this little escapade.

'Well, it's crazy isn't it?' she burst out as they strode along. 'We're mad kow-towing to a girl who's simply got a chip on her shoulder and who thinks the whole world revolves round herself. I've tried to be sympathetic . . . but I just don't seem able to say anything right to her . . .'

'A simple question of being beloved, old sport,' came the cheerful reply . . . 'and the unrequitedness thereof. Buck up. We're having a stunning wheeze. Maud's an ass, but she's given us a pretty good excuse for an adventure. Tell us again what happened after the match.'

It was Jennifer speaking, and as they linked arms Alison shot her a pretty hard look. Somehow she'd imagined these other two had put aside the matter of the motor car incident. Apparently they had not. Perhaps they were not as frivolous as they might at first appear. Even though she'd already explained the bare bones of the case Alison found herself again searching those cheery faces.

'Come on,' Jen coaxed. 'Spit out what's going on? You're all het up and we want to know why. What's the matter old aching heart? Mm. You see, we think we spotted those men on the hockey field.'

'Oh lor.' Alison dabbed her forehead. They had arrived in the village but all the curtains were drawn across the lamplit windows. No one else seemed fond enough of moonlight to enjoy the keen night air. So the three adventurers fled across the street and opened the gate to the woodland path without interruption. As they settled down to a brisk climb Alison admitted: 'Yes, they *were* there. They popped up behind a bush at exactly the wrong moment, waving their bit of paper.'

'That *wasn't* from your dad?'

'No I'm sure it wasn't,' she decided firmly.

'Then what on earth *do* they want?'

Alison bit her lip.

'I'd like to be able to tell you,' she muttered, 'but I can't because I don't know myself. Honestly Hil, I can't tell you any more than I've already explained.'

She did know a little more of course. She knew they wanted the box. But it was what was *in* that box that mattered. Until *that* was known, she was as much in the dark as they were.

'Oh well,' Hilary laughed, 'we'll find out sooner or later I suppose. Must have put you completely off your stroke though.'

'It did.'

Their curiosity now aroused, the two faces craned to wrest any information they could get out of her.

'You say Miss *Devine* claimed to know them? I must admit I find *that* pretty incredible. They were such queer and *seedy* creatures, weren't they?'

Alison agreed. 'Yes; it's a puzzle.'

Owls were hooting by the big trees and Jennifer looked up into interlacing boughs that were clearly silhouetted against a bright sky. She shivered.

'I only hope they aren't here now. We wouldn't stand a chance.'

And certainly there were plenty of places for anyone to hide. The chums on the other hand were clearly visible, and with the black sea of pines looming they began to feel their vulnerability. How the woods seemed to press down on them now with a frowning sternness as if displeased by their presence. The three found themselves breaking into a gallop.

Although there were high odds against anyone being hidden in this remote fastness, the feeling that someone *might* be quite close to them . . . even a poacher . . . had turned what had begun as a 'lark' into a bit of a nightmare. Secretly the 'twins' began to wish they were after all tucked up in their beds.

'Not far now,' Hilary assured them cheerfully. 'I *still* wouldn't want to be anywhere else.'

'Quite right old thing,' Jennifer agreed stoutly. 'Wouldn't have missed it for worlds.'

They had at last come, breathing rather heavily, to the

little knoll and Jennifer scrambled up its steep sides in the shadow.

'Golly; we must be cracked doing this,' she admitted, slithering back for the fourth time on to the others. 'I'm absolutely *covered* with mud,' she complained, looking down at her hands and dressing gown, as all three of them achieved the summit of the rocky projection.

But Hilary was not listening; for from the rise ahead she would catch her first view of the haunted ruins. It was something she was not looking forward to. Although outwardly so casual, Hilary was actually the most timid of the three girls. Of all the bogeys in her private world (and there were plenty) the things she feared most were 'spooks'. And if there was any single place more than any other, where ghosts were most likely to be seen . . . that place was the castle in the woods above Coxeley Grange.

Hilary was suddenly afraid. A drear sight on the sunniest of days, what the ruins would look like now did not bear thinking about.

'Oh my sainted aunt,' gasped Jennifer. 'Am I potty, or is that a light?'

'Where? Where? I can't see anything?'

'No . . . because you've got your eyes shut you silly goof. Over there through that little window; and it's moving about.'

Hilary risked one quick look at last, then clung to her friends.

The moon was as bright as day. Across the smooth lawns, fingers of shadows reached out from the looming towers and hanging crenellated masonry, spreading almost to their feet. But what petrified them most was another smaller source of illumination at the base of the great bastion of stone that lay so silently sihouetted against the night sky. Through a slit in the wall, a light was almost certainly flickering.

'Oh lor,' breathed Jennifer. 'Isn't it creepy?'

'More creepy than anything I've ever seen,' Hilary breathed without reservation. 'D'you think we might slip back now, actually?'

'No . . . wait a minute . . . It's queer.' This was Alison making the same unnerving request as she'd done the last time they were here . . . and both 'twins' inwardly groaned. The girl turned to them, eager and alive. 'If there's something spooky going on, I want to find out what it is. Let's nip over there.'

'What?' hooted Hilary aghast. 'You mean you actually want to *see*?'

'Of course I want to see. Don't you? This is a *dare* isn't it?'

'Oh fishcakes, of course.' Jennifer wiped her brow with her sleeve. 'All right Macduff. Lead on.'

Once again it was the one who'd pooh-poohed the whole affair who was now taking command of the situation, as she seemed destined always to do.

Half walking, half gliding, quiet as a ghost, Alison led the way across the still bright grass, to the edges of the rearing ruin itself, to a great gaping hole of an entrance that opened under the main tower like the mouth of a cave. Thwarted in her previous attempts at exploration, all the adventurous spirit of the Daynes was now aroused. The other two had fallen in behind their natural leader – Hilary with a hanky already stuffed into her mouth, just in case there might be a temptation to scream. Cautiously, they entered the black space. A sudden whirl of disturbed bats swarmed squeaking round their faces, and Hilary bit her hanky as she ducked to avoid an entangling of tiny claws. Oh jiminy . . . this was dreadful.

The way became a passage; with large stones poking out of the floor, and much more hazardous. But with the torch now bravely agleam, the blackness behind them kept Hil and Jen as close as possible to their pilot. With infinite care Alison now sidled to a corner of stone and slowly peered round. ('Oh I don't know how you dared,' Hilary declared afterwards.) The way had become wider there, and inexplicably lighter. There was a pale yellow glow, an unaccountable source of illumination and in another moment Hilary would have fled – stumbling, cutting her shins on the rocks, anything to get out of this dreadful place. Suddenly she too saw . . .

In a niche in the roughly hewn stonework stood a single guttering candle. A tramp! They sighed with relief. Just a measly old tramp. At last now they were free to retreat in honour and run back to school as fast as their legs would carry them. Silently, pleadingly, Hilary tried to pull her friends from this awful hole, but that wretched Alison was again for some unknown reason resisting.

Mercy . . . she was standing there like a stuffed owl, gazing at something on the floor over in the corner. In fact, she had even begun to urge them forward and now was slowly, delicately, silently approaching, then bending down over . . . a pair of projecting boots . . . a pair of men's boots! – poking from a pile of sacking and Alison was going to . . . she had *done* it! She had whipped away the sacks from . . . *nothing*! The boots sagged slowly over and fell. Then Hilary screamed.

The sound came piercingly and rebounded, echoing from wall to wall, as, without warning, a hand descended on her shoulder.

'What are you doing here?' The boyish voice sounded peeved, rather mildly indignant. But as Hilary came gropingly back to life it was Alison who incredulously exploded.

'It's only a *boy*. How dare you jump out like that? Release her at once.' Such indignation was quite silly and unwarranted as afterwards she was the first to admit. Of course Hilary could easily have wriggled away if she'd wanted to, in spite of a grip that seemed to be pressing on a paralysing shoulder nerve and keeping her stuck there. But the relief at finding this bespectacled earnest youth who might have been a schoolboy brother to any one of them . . . had been just too great for silence.

As it happened, the bespectacled figure never flinched. 'Not,' said the boy reasonably, 'until I know who you are and where you've come from.' The tone was level . . . *firm*.

'We're from St Ursula's School for Girls, and we're on a dare.' This was Jennifer, poutily replying. 'Who are you?'

'Stephen Devine.'

The shock produced by this simple answer was something they'd never get over, not even, said Hilary, if they lived to be a hundred.

'Stephen *Devine*?'

They had suffered much en route. Their legs were scratched, thick mud encrusted their feet and with their hands and bodies icy cold, the explorers were more tired than any would have cared to admit. But this was an extraordinary statement – and it electrified them. The youth might just as credibly claim to be the King. And here came another shock. For perfectly calmly Alison affirmed:

'Then you must be Miss Devine's brother.'

'What?' Jennifer cried. 'He's too young.'

That was the really worrying thing, the fact that Miss Devine could have a brother so. . . so totally puny; not the fact that he'd been sleeping, as he so evidently had, under a pile of old sacks in a haunted ruin, and living on nuts and berries.

The fact that Alison *knew* . . . well that was something that had escaped them in the heat of the moment, but now the girl really stunned the twinsome pair:

'She's been ever so worried.'

'Who? Miss Devine?'

'Yes.'

'How do you know?'

'She told me.'

'*Told* you . . .' Hilary gasped.

Was Maud then right? Did Alison and their jealously guarded Headmistress really share a secret? The notion took a lot of swallowing. Why *Alison*? Why not one of them? Stephen explained:

'I ran away from school. Slansky was after me. I've been trying desperately to get to my sister but I know he's been spying on St Ursula's too. I can't risk it.'

Suddenly the matter had become clear. How churlish to have suspected their true friend. The qualms of jealous dismay subsided from Hilary as quickly as they'd come.

'Those men!' she burst out. 'He's talking about those dreadful men.'

Alison reached for an arm. 'Come on,' she said briskly to the boy. 'We'll take you back.'

'No. I shan't come.'

He pulled away from her, cowering and cringing. Momentarily disconcerted, Alison blew her nose. Thinking about it, perhaps he was right to stay. He'd been safe here up to now. The thing was simply to remain as inconspicuous as possible until they could get back and tell Miss Devine.

'Well if you won't come, you won't; but keep your lamp hidden Stephen, or those ghastly men *will* find you . . .' She replaced the hanky in her pocket and prepared to leave. 'We'll tell your sister directly we get back.' Then came the next vexation.

'She's not *there*, Ali,' Hilary revealed. 'Didn't you know?'

'No.'

'Probably gone to see his Headmaster,' Jennifer conjectured in a flash of inspiration.

'She won't be back till late tomorrow afternoon,' Hilary explained . . . 'I know because Peggy was told she'd have to miss her music lesson and Peggy told Tryphena . . .'

'You can't stay here all *that* time,' said Alison, horrified.

'I can,' the boy declared stoutly, 'and I will.'

'D'you have anything to eat?'

'Only blackberries . . .'

'What?'

Their voices trailed away.

'I really don't want anything,' he urged gently.

Who *was* this outlandish brother who would rather starve than risk capture? And who were the men that so threatened him?

'I've got a couple of rather furry cakes from the feast in my pocket,' Hilary announced, practical as always.

'And here's some chocolate,' Jennifer added kindly. 'It's my last bit but you can have it.'

'Oh, thanks awfully . . .'

The boy snatched the gifts and crammed them greedily into his mouth as they watched . . . fur and all.

They were spot on, these girls, Alison decided . . . so instinctively heartwarmingly right in whatever they did. How satisfying to have them beside her at this crucial moment. Alison suddenly knew that, through all the unexplained events, a thread ran that linked them, all four.

It was good to have chums. If these two had not so unquestioningly accepted Maud's challenge, none of them would have been here now. And Stephen might have starved to death without Miss Devine even knowing. There came a welling up of gratitude. All the difficulties of the term had been a trial of strength for unknown tasks ahead. Now she need never be alone again. How *could* she, when here beside her, sharing the mystery, were the two best chums ever?

As they prepared to go, Stephen unexpectedly crumbled.

'Don't leave me.' His pleading voice was quite pathetic, a little boy's again.

'We've got to I'm afraid,' Jennifer informed him reasonably. 'We can't stay here all night.'

'Oh, please don't go.'

For a long moment they peered at him. Then Hilary said gently: 'We'll be back tomorrow and your sister . . . our Head . . . your sister'll come too.'

Still the boy stared pleadingly at them.

'Maybe,' stumbled Alison finally, 'maybe we should tell Miss Prosser?'

If the other two almost leapt into the air yelping, 'Oh no!' . . . the boy's horror seemed even more intense!

'Don't,' he cried, owl eyes blinking behind those round serious spectacles. 'Don't tell anyone else at all. It's desperate and vital you speak only to my sister.' He paused, looking tired and defeated then added cheerlessly: 'I'll wait here till tomorrow night.'

'Well do keep out of sight Stephen,' Hilary urged . . . 'from that terrible person. What did you say his name was?'

'Slansky. Count Slansky. Till tomorrow night then.'

'Good heavens,' Hilary was gasping, as they half hopped, half ran out into the open air. 'Could you have ever dreamt of such a thing? I mean Miss Devine having such a little tick for a brother. It's not right . . . I mean, she's so beautiful and he's so . . . ticklike . . . a sort of worried bird.'

'Don't keep on about it,' Alison replied wearily.

'An owl,' said Jennifer.

'Yes, a kind of owl and why should an owl have got it into his head that he's so jolly important? Why's this Count Slansky sleuthing *him* I want to know? I mean . . . who'd want to? I certainly wouldn't.'

Alison, who as usual had other ideas, barely heard any of the conversation, which ran on similar lines all the way back to the school. Not that she too did not think about Stephen.

'I feel so awfully sorry for him,' she ventured. 'His clothes looked so thin. Perhaps I should have lent him my dressing gown?'

Hilary turned aghast.

'Wha-at? And risk being questioned by *that woman*? She'd be bound to squeeze the truth out of us then.'

Oh, those prophetic words, born of long and bitter experience.

The returning adventurers felt drained and weary. The moon had reached its zenith and its rays streamed brightly out of a cold sky. The intrepid three lost any interest they might have had in the moon, and now at last with the silent and stately pile of St Ursula's homing into view, their pace quickened.

The fire escape was deep in the shadow of the looming walls, so they were obliged to file by torchlight up the long metal stairs that led to the topmost floor of the building and to the warmth and safety of their own little dormitory, their home under the eaves.

Home . . . Until that night Alison would have laughed at the idea of calling school 'home'. Tonight, for the first time, she felt differently. Somehow tonight's escapade had introduced a new dimension into this queer business they called school life and that they all had to accept without question. Even a prisoner sometimes in the end begins to like his cell. Whether or not any similarity can be seen in the two situations, there remains one abiding truth. Better to accept and yield . . . to jolly well make the best of a bad job . . . and then it might turn out to be not so bad after all.

Though she'd never listened her father had told her this over and over again. Now their adventure together made her realize that her coming to school had not been simply a matter of convenience to her father. Maths she might hate, Latin she might be a complete dud at, but there was something else about St Ursula's – a spirit of camaraderie that taught you to give and take with the rest, to make allowances for those weaker than yourself and even for those apparently much stronger . . . even Prosser.

Comradeship. It was something she'd only ever experienced with her father. She'd had friends, but never anyone like Jen or Hil; and now, as they approached in darkness the end of the stairway and its little door leading to their welcoming dormitory, she felt as if she were indeed coming home. The warriors were returning victorious to the old school, no longer as three separate individuals but a single battle unit.

Now they reached the very topmost step and, with her hand on the doorhandle, Alison swung her torch round straight into the face of . . . Miss Prosser. For a moment the actors in a real life play stood paralysed as the ghastly mask hung there, a white staring face silhouetted in the encircling black. Then the door snatched open.

'*So* Alison Dayne,' the metallic voice cried out, 'you presume to take advantage of your Headmistress's absence?'

Mercy . . . Glory . . . she was guilty again. Guilt. Guilt. She was deeply and inherently guilty.

'How dare you?' came the detested voice. 'How *dare* you? Never in my long years at this school have I encountered a more wilful and disagreeable girl than you. I shall recommend your expulsion forthwith.'

A terrible feeling of guilt gripped Alison. Expulsion? She must be as wicked as Prosser claimed. She was going to be expelled!

One lone voice piped up in her defence. It was a small voice in the corner (not Maud Willison's of course) saying:

'Here, hang on a mo Miss Prosser. Alison's not the only one to be blamed.' The mistress turned her freezing glare, switching its icy beam from Alison for a moment, to someone within.

'Do not be impertinent madam.' There was a pause . . . and then as though as an afterthought: 'As for you others, punishment will be selected tomorrow afternoon on Miss Devine's return.'

The mistress pulled back the fire escape door, allowing the errant three to enter. Hanging their heads, they filed past the heavily breathing presence and over to their beds. After another explosive glare around the room, their mentor closed the fire escape door. She locked and bolted it. Then she marched across the polished linoleum and left the room.

For a long time after the door into the corridor had closed with a click, the three offenders lay petrified in their beds. At last somebody managed to bring her thoughts to the surface.

'Satisfied now Maud are you?'

But the reply that emerged as a sigh came from someone else . . . certainly not from Maud's now very still corner place.

'Oh let the little worm alone,' said this person in resignation. 'She'll never know what it is she's done.'

'Miss Prosser. I am convinced you cannot run a school under a system of martial law!'

The speaker was Miss Devine, and the place the Head-mistress's study. Behind that closed door a discussion was raging. That it was raging rather than merely progressing had already been made abundantly clear. The voices bore none of that calmness that normally characterizes such exchanges between school mistresses. Indeed, from the ringing tone of Miss Prosser's reply, all courtesies seemed to have been abandoned long ago and thrown, like chaff, to the four winds.

Had there *ever* been harmony between these two ladies who held joint responsibility for the smooth running of the school? It seemed unlikely, for in the second mistress's sneering accusations there clanged a jarring note of recklessness that bordered on personal insult. To this latest assertion she uttered a short dismissive laugh.

'Pah!' she hooted derisively. 'Whoever suggested such a thing? This case is different. I am speaking about a quite flagrant act of disobedience on the part of one girl who . . .'

The second in command at St Ursula's was not allowed to finish. The injustice was apparently too much for Miss Devine and the spirit and gusto of her interruption warmed the hearts of the nervous gathering outside her door. Her objection had emerged quite clearly:

'You may still yet be mistaken,' she had icily retorted. The war was *not* yet over.

'But I think not,' came the hammering reply, its conviction unwavering. 'I simply wish to state . . .' (and Prosser stated) . . . 'that I have my source of information.'

'Then may *I* state,' flared Miss Devine, 'that I am inclined to regard your source as shabby, if not despicable.'

In the public schools of England the idea of 'sneaks' has always caused great alarm. People refrain from giving away the names of their comrades, however much they may despise them. They do not go immediately running to authority with tales of woe. So Miss Devine's caustic rejoinder and its insulting imputation was perfectly clear to Prosser. And if there had been an opportunity for a timid knock at the door by the eavesdroppers outside, it had now passed.

'Miss Devine,' Miss Prosser launched . . . the voice had lowered to a menacing snarl . . . 'unlike yourself, I have been in the teaching profession for nearly thirty-two years and for twenty of those at this school. Never, never, have I had my authority flouted in such a manner.'

She may have been talking about Alison. On the other hand she may have meant Miss Devine herself . . .

'Oh golly!'

It was the turn of the 'twins' now to look aghast. Hilary turned towards her two companions. She and Jen had come with news so startling, it had successfully choked off their worst fears for themselves.

It should have been news to soothe the taut and anxious face of their adored Headmistress, and make it pretty again. Now things looked hopeless. In exerting the deadly pressure that had for so long kept her successfully at the top of the St Ursula's teaching staff, Prosey was as usual spoiling everything.

Nerves racked, the waiting chums listened. They listened in the greatest anxiety for that which must surely soon decide their fate. It came at last.

'I am sorry Miss Prosser,' – Miss Devine's reply was firm – 'but I insist.' There was a pause while the listeners subsided in relief. 'I must be allowed to deal with this matter in my own way. Where are those wretched girls?'

The obedient knock was instant.

'Come in.'

The girls trooped inside. Hanging their heads, they ranged themselves before the desk of judgement.

'Hilary, Jennifer, Alison. What can I do but express my

75

utter disappointment? You must realize that a Headmistress who finds one of her girls untrustworthy cannot from then on regard that girl as she does the others. Now Miss Prosser here informs me that *you* Alison were the ringleader in this escapade . . .'

'Oh Miss Devine,' Hilary burst out, 'that isn't true. She didn't even want to go.'

Miss Prosser's reply was as scathing as boiling water.

'Rubbish girl. It's useless trying to protect your comrade.'

Wearily, Miss Devine sighed.

'Miss Prosser. Might not the ethics of schoolgirl honour fruitfully be left for discussion on another occasion?'

To this, the second mistress merely clicked her tongue, turning with a gesture of impatience towards the wall. But however irrelevant Hilary's outcry may have seemed to Miss Prosser, for Alison it was of supreme importance and she glanced gratefully at her trusty friend. Too many times since her arrival at St Ursula's she had been punished for offences she was unaware of committing.

The fact that the new girl had become Miss Prosser's pet hate was no secret in the school. Alison's form mates had helped her too often with lines to be left in doubt. No one questioned the unfairness of the repeated attacks, or the ludicrous bias of the sarcasm and spite. *Why* Alison should have been thus selected was a mystery discussed from the first form to the mighty sixth. Surely Maud was only part of the reason? They all agreed on one point . . . that Prosser's view of the new fourth former was entirely unjustified. What mattered now was whether the Head had reached the same conclusion. Failure at maths was one thing . . . midnight adventures quite another.

What an opportunity for Prossy to be rid of her avowed enemy for ever! Even now the chums could see hope rising in that skinny breast as the second mistress awaited her superior's decision.

'All that remains is the choice of punishment,' came Miss Devine's sombre voice. Prosser's eyes gleamed. Alison trembled in the knees. 'In view of the circumstances, I propose to place all three of you on . . . silence week.'

Whatever that might be, it did not sound like expulsion. There was silence now. The second mistress appeared about to expire. For a while her mouth opened and closed like a fish's but then she found her voice at last.

'Is that *all*?' she screeched.

'Certainly that is all,' came the Head's measured response. 'Considering the nature of the misconduct, I think being forbidden for seven days to leave the grounds must be wholly appropriate. And girls, listen . . . for seven days you will speak only amongst yourselves . . . to no other girl for any reason whatever. Miss Prosser. I must apologize. I have a splitting headache. You may all go.'

Speechless, the second mistress stood rooted to the spot. She could not have been more amazed had she just been listening to a judge acquit a murderer and her legs simply refused to move.

But then with a jolt of anger she jerked herself into motion and walked unsteadily towards the exit. Hilary even opened the door for her. With a final withering glare round the offenders, the woman strode from the room and away down the passage like a disappointed vulture.

The girls too found themselves departing from that hallowed chamber without having had the nerve to gasp out even a hint of their secret. Their knees were knocking and their hearts contrite. They were grateful with a gratitude that for the moment overwhelmed them. As they clustered again round the door, the hated batlike figure flapped on its way to the last lesson of the day (to the fifth as it happened) . . . but the frowning chums bent their heads to the task in hand.

'Well,' said Hilary. 'What do we do?'

'Knock of course.'

Miss Devine was just rearranging some flowers. Jennifer had been correct about the reason for the Head's temporary absence from school. But when Miss Devine had finally spoken to Stephen's Headmaster, it was to find she had drawn a blank. He knew absolutely nothing of the boy's whereabouts. He had not the slightest idea what had made the boy run away. All he could suggest was that they contact the police. At Miss Devine's specific request, he had been forced against his better judgement to refrain from this course, but by now his temper was beginning to show distinct signs of wear and tear. Indeed the interview had concluded in a most unsatisfactory manner, leaving Miss Devine in something like despair.

Frustrated and exhausted she had then received abysmal service at the only hotel in the small country town. Her dinner had been cold and she had not even touched the breakfast. She had barely slept a wink.

Now she toyed with soothing flowers, for of all the blessings given by a merciful providence to calm the fevered mind, flowers are the best.

She had not the slightest doubt as to what had happened. The Count, as she had already told Alison, was an old enemy. Since the day he had leant ingratiatingly over her little brother's wooden cot, the boy had been terrified even by Slansky's name. According to Stephen, he had awoken on that occasion to a full view of the narrowing eyes and cruel leering mouth, and swore he had heard the following muttered threat:

'It's either you or me my boy. One day you know . . . I shall have to destroy you.'

It had taken Slansky five years to pay this first visit to his nephew, but from that day the boy had lived in a state of terror for an uncle he had fortunately rarely seen since. Now the ogre had come back. And with the crisis in the Balkans reaching international proportions, Stephen evidently felt he had come to fulfil his threat . . . and his sister shivered for the seedy child she had striven so long and so hard to protect.

She must keep calm. She had to keep telling herself this one thing. For if the boy died, it would be her fault. She should have acted on that first day barely one week ago when Alison had first unwittingly drawn the evil dictator's offensive presence to the school. She should have phoned Stephen's Headmaster directly there and then and had Stephen sent here where at least she could guard him herself. There could be no search. The police were out of the question. Hers was not a plight for public ears . . . not anyway until all those loose threads had been tied together at last. Only then would the world know their secret, and that moment seemed further away now then it had ever been.

For all *she* knew, Stephen might be lying at this moment in a ditch with a razor through his throat and the old familiar sign of the Kyasht carved into his poor bare chest. Oh *how* she inwardly shuddered as she touched and primped those autumn blooms. No . . . she could not relax . . . Then there came a tap at the door and she found herself actually snapping:

'Come in.'

The three girls who had just left came filing into the room again.

Now Miss Devine was fully aware of her responsibilities and her duty as a leader and a guide to the unwary. But she felt singularly let down by these three girls. In her absence they had failed her. Alison had of course been led by the other two. What they had done was after all not so very bad . . . such high jinks being simply an extension of the hockey fever which occasionally struck the school. Yet she found herself almost shouting:

'Hilary? Jennifer? Alison? . . . What is it now?'

Shamefacedly they hung their heads. Jennifer nudged Hilary who, spokesman as usual, blurted out:

'Miss Devine . . . firstly we are most tremendously *sorry* for what we did . . .'

The Head's manner subsided. She bit her lip. They were only children.

'I most sincerely hope you *are* sorry . . . not just because it has meant punishment but because you realize how much your behaviour has been a grief to me.'

They *did* know. And faced with this gentle woman so pale and wan, how deeply they regretted that foolish act. Yet their news felt hot inside, burning their tongues from being so long held back.

'Oh, golly yes . . .' Hilary burst out, her face alight . . . 'But there's something else, something really important. When we were at the old castle last night, we discovered a boy.' She gulped and got ready for the revelation. 'His name was . . . Stephen Devine.'

Miss Devine caught her breath. But as Hilary's eyes continued to blaze into hers with such fervid intensity, the blood that had been wildly coursing in her ears stopped buzzing and she replied with incredulity:

'Stephen? Did you say . . . Stephen?'

'But yes,' they all three cried in unison, their eager faces alight with pleasure.

'Oh . . . thank Heaven.'

It was all the mistress could manage to blurt out. Passing a hand over her brow, she sank unsteadily into her chair.

'But he wants us to tell you,' Jennifer urged frantically, 'that his life is in mortal danger . . .'

'From someone called Count Slansky.'

'And having got as far as the ruins, he says he daren't come any further. He'll be starving by now . . .'

'Oh my dears . . .'

Miss Devine swung round. Impulsively she turned to take the two pairs of outstretched hands into her own with all her characteristically spontaneous warmth. Her lips were parted and her eyes alight.

For a moment, Alison felt great happiness for Jennifer and Hilary. They had been forgiven and she felt almost envious . . . certainly wistful. *They* had not been branded ringleaders . . . The Head was young and beautiful again.

'*Someone*'ll have to go and fetch him,' she was declaring. '*I* certainly don't know that I trust myself to find a path through those woods at night.'

'Oh . . . we know the way,' Jennifer assured her.

Miss Devine uttered a low musical laugh.

'I'm sure you do.' Her eyes twinkled . . . 'But I can hardly allow all of you to go. The absence of three such notorious reprobates en masse wouldn't stay unnoticed for long. This is a matter of the greatest delicacy. At all costs Stephen's presence in the school must remain unperceived.'

'But *why*?' Jennifer burst out. 'What on earth is going on?'

'*You*,' said Hilary impulsively to Alison . . . 'you must do it Ali.'

Hilary glanced at her adored Headmistress and the lady nodded. Alison jerked back into life. They couldn't really mean *her*? . . . not when they were really dancing to do the thing themselves. That would indeed be sacrifice.

'Oh, Hil!' she cried. 'You can't mean it?'

'Of *course* I mean it. Honestly . . . you were so nice to the boy and so level headed . . .'

'Oh yes,' Jennifer instantly agreed, and her voice could not have been cheerier. 'He'd come back with you Alison.' The infinitely touching thing was, they actually *meant* it. 'There's nothing I'd like better than another expedish, especially a legal one and so on . . . but we're not motherly like you, dearest thing. He was distinctly suspicious of me, I know.'

With her arms slipped through theirs, Alison hugged them each quickly. Miss Devine was at her desk.

'I'll write him a little note. And if you, Jennifer, would send the prefect in charge of preparation to my study, I'll make some excuse about Alison's absence.'

'You mean you want me to go *now*?'

Miss Devine finished scribbling the note and handed it to her.

'Yes. Stay as inconspicuous as possible.'

'If you don't want him to be noticed, Stephen ought to be dressed just like Alison.' Jennifer spoke eagerly.

'Indeed. Wear your macintosh, my dear, and take one also for him. And be sure to lift the hoods.' Glancing nervously through the window, the Head clasped her hands. 'The mist is already rising. Take wellingtons. With water dripping from the trees, the leaves underfoot will be damp and slippery.'

'And don't you think they should avoid the village altogether?'

'Undoubtedly. Leave by the garden and when you return . . . hopefully completely unnoticed by those men, come in by the tradesmen's entrance.'

The group now moved to the door.

As Alison mentally prepared herself for her mission, Hilary emitted a heart rending sigh.

'Oh well Jen . . . I s'pose that's the end of *our* part in all this fearful excitement?'

Miss Devine laughed gaily.

'I think we might stretch a point and permit you both to share in the reunion. After all . . . if it hadn't been for that unmistakably "twinnish" brand of wickedness . . .' Her eyes twinkled.

'Oh Miss Devine,' Hilary burst out, 'you are a brick. Didn't

81

I say it to you Ali? Didn't I tell you that very first day on the train, how absolutely top hole and ripping she was?'

'Flattery, Miss Marchant,' the young Headmistress giggled, 'will get you nowhere at all.' Could there in that happy moment be any doubt that the reunion would take place? 'The punishment stands as before. Silence indeed may be more than golden just now.'

CHAPTER

11

Unhappily, the first setback came almost immediately. It was simply a link in a chain of events that was to literally shake St Ursula's to its very foundations and to find for Alison a permanent place in the annals of the old school's history.

Contrary to Miss Prosser's recently so forcibly expressed opinion, Alison Dayne had no wish to hold the limelight. Not for her the attractions of strutting about the fourth form common room as had many a schoolgirl goddess before . . . puffing her chest out with affectation in front of the admiring crowd.

And if this particular collusion *did* happen to be with the most romantic of all Headmistresses, then that too was something to be taken, like any other task, in her stride. Though she was able to rejoice with Miss Devine about the discovery of her brother, for Alison there was another aspect of the mystery . . .

She had never for one moment forgotten her little gold box, nestling in the conservatory. Every day she had checked that it was still there in the soil. Not for the first time had she felt the cool conviction that the trinket somehow lay not only at the root of an enormous lily, but also at the root of every single curious thing that had happened during this eventful term. Slansky wanted that box. He was not going to *find* her treasure – not if she could help it. But if Slansky wanted it . . . then the box had something to do with Stephen. And if Slansky wanted *Stephen* . . . then Stephen had something to do with the box.

One imponderable remained and that was the extent of her present danger.

Assuredly they were hiding somewhere round the school, those two malefactors. They were waiting for someone. They were waiting in fact for *her*. These two villains were intent on delivering a letter, ostensibly from her father. It was one she had no wish to receive, and the important thing at this moment was to keep out of their sight. *That* all depended on being able to slip away like a shadow now, as with bag and torch at the ready, she ran full tilt down the steps to the school's least used exit. Here was to be found the junior cloakroom, the much used chamber that, smelling so familiarly of macs and wellies, reminded her more poignantly than any other place in the school of home.

She could not waste time on such soppy thoughts now, as pulling on her own mac and stuffing Jennifer's into the bag (Jennifer being the bigger of the other two girls) she rose straight into the face of Maud. For a moment the two stared at each other. How *did* that girl move so quietly about? She *was* a spy, a real one, and for a moment Alison's eyes dilated in horror. But the disquiet lasted only a second for the scholarship 'creep' had begun to whine:

'Forgive me Alison. I'm really sorry for making you go out on that dare. I love you. I honestly do!'

Well *that* was just as well, and Alison sighed with relief. She was just about to reassure her classmate when she remembered – silence week. She could just hear Miss Devine's voice, the actual words in her head . . . 'and remember girls, you are to speak only among yourselves and to no other girl on any account whatever.'

Let us not accuse Alison of taking matters too literally . . . of being perhaps just a trifle naïve. Let's say instead that in the traditions of the Dayne family there was a born respect of the law that brooked no compromise. Right was right . . . and wrong? Well – her father's commands she had always simply taken as gospel.

So it was for the honour of St Ursula's that Alison on this occasion, and so unfortunately as it turned out, forbore to reply to a cry from the heart of the loneliest girl in the school.

Simply placing finger to lips, Alison gazed at Maud with an entreaty she desperately hoped would be understood. Of course, it was not.

Now Maud had never since her very first day got used to ways and manners she found both baffling and unreal. Not for her the mysterious logic of 'the code'. For this thing that had been founded with the very school itself sprang from girls with a completely different background . . . generations of such cherubs to whom correct behaviour came automatically. Silence week was something Maud had never heard of. She was flummoxed. Indeed she was more than flummoxed. She was snubbed again.

With that ready anger that would always dog her steps, she found her voice at last.

'Alison? Where are you going?' She clung to the arm of the beloved with a crablike grip. 'You're not *listening*,' she insisted furiously. 'Why don't you speak to me?'

Alison was not going to speak to her. She had promised not to speak to anyone. With a final glare of despair, the embarrassed sleuth dragged herself free and made for the door. It was not an auspicious beginning to her mission.

Maud's reaction was immediate. It had cost the girl a good deal to make that apology to Alison. She'd been biting her nails about it all day. Now she'd had the words simply flung back in her face. Retaliation was unavoidable. Her eyes flashed. Even now, straining to see what was happening, she could scarcely believe what those eyes saw as they peered out over the garden. Alison was running down towards the garden gate. What happened next must be sheer perversity. Alison Dayne had opened the gate. She was about to perform the unthinkable and leave the school!

The fact that beyond the gate lay the potting shed, the bicycle store, the conservatory and the whole of the vegetable garden, did not occur to Maud now. Alison had her mac on. That was enough. Not satisfied apparently with the results of last night's fiasco, this Dayne girl had decided to defy authority and was actually breaking the bounds *again*. For a moment Maud ceased to believe her prying eyes. Her mind whirled. When her mind whirled she thought little about repercussions. Indeed she thought of nothing at all at such moments beyond what she had seen or heard.

The girl from the north habitually acted on impulse. Within St Ursula's code she could be accused of being a sneak. Here at St Ursula's, let us simply say that in Miss Prosser the isolated child had found a ready ear for any small confidences that might lead to an easier life for both of them, and that she'd fallen into this way because no one had bothered to suggest any other, not even Alison. For Alison, who had been Maud's unwitting goddess – the ideal to which she aspired – had had just too much on her mind that term.

For Alison, as luck would have it, Maud's sudden craning presence at the top of the topiary garden steps could not have been more fortunate. For at the bespectacled pupil's appearance, two strange 'gardeners' who had suddenly bobbed up over a hedge to observe Alison's movements were forced to bob down again out of sight. Now with the garden gate quietly closing and Alison going about her mysterious business, Maud hesitated no longer. Her reaction was swift and to the point.

Several seconds after, with the conservatory door open, probing fingers might have been seen dipping into the soil of one particularly large plant pot.

A short while later, unluckily for the two 'gardeners', a third figure appeared at those most popular of garden steps. Instant pursuit was suddenly out of the question. All day they had waited and now this strange creature had appeared to frustrate the capture of the girl they so keenly wished to interview.

They had no choice but to remain hidden. There was no brooking the livid countenance they now beheld. Under the hat that had been rammed on at a moment's notice, the face resembled one of those celebrated Gorgons of Greek mythology that so terrified the bold Odysseus. Even the Gorgons themselves might have paled in that unnerving moment, and Slansky remained paralysed behind his bush.

Hair loose, clothes anyhow, the second mistress gave voice. It had taken twenty years for a girl to get so totally under her skin.

'Alison Dayne . . . you wicked girl,' she shrieked. 'Come back!'

86

And as the lady took to her heels in screeching, full blooded pursuit, the Count and his companion exchanged fearful glances. A new understanding passed between them at that moment.

CHAPTER
12

To Alison, the wild unearthly cries sounded faintly, as but a throb in the air. They could have been the cry of a tawny owl hunting in the cool stillness of the misty dusk that, after her departure from school, had immediately wrapped her in its all enveloping protection.

She had by now, with the blood fairly singing in her veins, fled away from the gate in the wall that marked the school boundaries and out into open country.

Marshy to begin with, dotted with dying flag and hardy sedge, this was a deliberately confusing route. She avoided the conventional path to the ruins. Crossing the low ground that drained the marshes, Alison chose instead a roundabout route to the wooded semi-circle of hills whose dark bulk frowned all around. Aware that she had well and truly bungled her exit from St Ursula's, there was no option now but to cross this unfamiliar ground.

In choosing her as their emissary however the 'twins' had been unerring. For she possessed an instinctive sense of direction. At heart a sleuth like her father, she was secret agent, rescuer and Miss Devine's devoted slave, all rolled into one. For a second she paused to sniff the air and her nostrils flared – just like old Nutkin's. This was unknown terrain. Danger lurked. Only once had she looked closely into the eyes of a really evil man. That once had been enough. It was with a wild sense of relief that she at last gained the shelter of the trees.

She loved the woods. They were to Alison now, as always, a place of refuge. As a child she had delighted in their mystery; in spring so mysteriously and so suddenly carpeted with bluebells, in winter silent under the enveloping snow. At this moment they were muffled by fog. The cloying pale vapour offered cover for all hunted creatures, and it was by the paths of deer, badger and fox that she was being led instinctively to her goal.

To say that Miss Prosser's feelings about woods were at variance with the above, is perhaps unnecessary. To Prosser, characteristically, all country places were equally repellent. Prossy was not a lover of nature. Not for her the delights of a first primrose nestling close to a mossy boulder.

To the clinical second mistress a flower was something worth scientific investigation. Its petals might be counted before being removed, but then they had to be thrown away in the rubbish bin. And if she'd ever taken any satisfaction in the glorious panorama that surrounded St Ursula's, be assured it was from the safety of the grounds.

Finding herself therefore suddenly in the semi-darkness of such hostile surroundings as lay beyond the school's furthermost garden gate, even *she* experienced a twinge of doubt regarding the wisdom of this full blooded pursuit. It did not however last long. Alison Dayne was somewhere out there – Alison Dayne who had to be instantly brought back to retribution and what must surely *this* time be final justice.

The necessity of the apprehending and subsequent removal of this blight from her life was now more pressing than any temporary discomfort. Taking it for granted that Alison had done the same, she followed the natural path. Because it ran by the river, it was of course muddy. But because it ran by the river, it was also out of bounds. Once a girl had lost her balance there and drowned. Miss Prosser hoped she would not be cheated of her own prey so easily.

After a while the path divided, one fork leading to the village; and this was the course Miss Prosser intended to pursue now. But in the half-light and her state of confusion the mistress chose the path that led . . . nowhere. So wrathful felt this upholder of right and justice, that she barely noticed *where* she was going. That any girl could quite so coolly and offhandedly choose again to break school rules, after punishment for exactly the same misconduct less than twenty-four hours previously . . . well, it was as outrageous as it was stupefying.

Above all the act showed contempt. It showed a total contempt, not merely for her own, but for *all* authority; and Miss Devine would soon be shown how wrong had been her judgement of that unspeakable vixen.

The Head's leniency in punishment was something that constantly galled Miss Prosser. If there was one thing Miss Prosser found *more* irritating, then it was that Miss Devine was Headmistress at all! It was well known in the school that, on the retirement of the former Head, Miss Prosser had been passed over by the governors in favour of the younger woman. That, she supposed bitterly, was all that could be expected of men. How its ignominious unfairness bit into her now, as the impeding briars scratched their hurtful message into her skinny and unprotected legs! And how she wished to break the bond that seemed to have so imperceptibly grown between girl and Headmistress.

Jealousy was not a word Miss Prosser acknowledged. But at least before the coming of her hated pupil there had been peace at St Ursula's. For some reason this girl had chosen to shatter that peaceful state, and it was with a blind savagery that Miss Prosser slashed at the brambles.

As she slashed, she pondered. She pondered on her own misfortunes and her impending retirement. She pondered on the way she was misunderstood and at times even, she felt sure, almost resented in the school. But most of all, she pondered about this wretched Alison Dayne. Why *did* she so choose to break the rules? Undoubtedly the girl was both deceitful and arrogant. But that was not in itself sufficient explanation, the mistress felt sure.

Perhaps on this occasion the offender had gone simply to post a letter in the village, hoping in this way to demonstrate her contempt. Or was there perhaps – and Miss Prosser's mind had suddenly filled with the wildest conjecture – some more sinister motive? Could it be (the thought struck a chill even in that hardened breast) that the girl smoked cigarettes and had sought to replenish supplies?

Or perhaps . . . No, not even Alison Dayne. But *yes* why not? With these motherless daughters of military men, anything was possible. Perhaps the girl was a secret drinker? Maybe she was in the habit of disappearing villagewards every

90

evening, in search of much needed ale? From the marsh came the croak of a disturbed heron. Miss Prosser had no ears for such protests.

The possibility of discovering this wretched child about the very act of raising a pint pot spurred on the hapless female towards, as she fondly supposed, the village and the Dog and Duck. Zealot and teetotaller both, the thought of someone so enjoying themselves when she was not about almost made her trip over a projecting root.

But by now she was deeply and inextricably enmeshed in these heartless woods and as she realized, looking up into the skein of branches above her head, quite impossibly lost. Hopelessly, savagely she called out:

'Alison . . . Alison Dayne? Where are you?'

Her words were swallowed in fog.

Wildly, wildly again and again she called that intolerable name. She darted hither. She darted thither. She ran, she leapt; she scrambled and lurched and then suddenly and without warning the ground seemed to give way beneath her feet. She took off, that gallant upholder of morals, in a glide that, for a moment, had her flying lightly through the air's dampness. Then she fell flat on her face in the mud.

Had she been there to see this startling thing, Alison Dayne would have undoubtedly been the first to rush to the assistance of her hapless pursuer.

But Alison was not there. Unaware of her mistress's misfortune, the girl had topped Barrow Banks, and was standing alert and watchful, staring at the ruins. Harsh caws of the last rooks settling down for the night came 'aak . . . aak' from the branches above, and Alison smiled up into the rookery. Flapping wings sounded against the boughs. The girl ran lightly across the grass.

No one, she was convinced, had seen her come. The jumble of stones stood deserted as before.

She ran up to the gaping hole in the masonry and called softly: 'Stephen? Stephen?' All was still and quiet. A pigeon flapped away in a startling whirr of wings; then she plunged into the blackness.

'Stephen!' she called again. 'It's me. Alison.'

No sound came. Then she was joined by a silent shadowy

figure. She switched on her torch.

'Where's my sister?'

'She sent me because I know the woods. Here's her note. Has anybody been here?' she asked as the boy peered closely and suspiciously at it through his lenses.

'Nobody. Not a soul.'

He screwed up the paper and stuffed it in his pocket. Alison felt suddenly inadequate.

'Come on Stephen. You must put on this macintosh and pretend to be a schoolgirl. And here's some plum cake . . . and a few jam tarts.'

The boy ate greedily, forcing the food into his mouth with both hands while Alison waited.

He drank the cool clean water she had collected in a bottle from a spring, at the last minute so as not to be weighed down. Then obediently he pulled on the disguising mac and the wellington boots . . . and was ready.

A casual poacher might have wondered at the approaching pair converging on him down the woodland path and conversing so earnestly in low voices. He would have seen a pair of schoolgirls and he might have laughed, thinking of the only girls' school in the district, and thought: 'Those two are going to be in for it.'

There was a reason for this earnestness. Alison was asking Stephen some very important questions.

'What actually made you run away? What actually *caused* you to do it in the first place?'

'I've told you. I saw Slansky.'

'You mean you recognized him?'

'Immediately. He always dresses the same. You must have seen his picture in the papers?'

'Yes,' Alison admitted. She had. 'But *where* did you see him?' she insisted. 'How did it happen? Was he hiding in your room?'

'No. I was coming back from rugger. I was coming out of the rugger field gates,' he told her perfectly evenly, 'when I suddenly spotted Slansky's car . . . you know . . . that open tourer he always affects wherever he goes.'

'Affects,' Alison thought to herself. 'That's a jolly adult word.' She clicked. That was what was so strange about this boy. Stephen was an adult in miniature.

'He brings it over with him on the boat, or so I've heard say,' Stephen was going on. 'I can't believe that myself. I think he hires an identical one over here when he picks up his English chauffeur. He's so keen on his image and makes no attempt to hide himself – not the least. Anyway, there he was, large as life, him and the chauffeur sitting with their backs to me, luckily. He *always* hires a chauffeur – that's the other thing – and I could see this one's eyes looking at me in the driving mirror. I didn't recognize him, but the queer thing is I felt sure somehow he recognized me. The chauffeur didn't do anything. He barely moved a muscle. Just an eyebrow flickered and then he lifted it quite slowly as though to say something. I bolted, I can tell you. I ran straight back to my study and collected a few things – my pebble collection you know and a few bus tickets – they're very rare ones. I got them up north mostly. It's so much nicer in England, up north . . .'

'Go on,' said Alison.

'Well then I dashed down to my locker and collected all my money. I always have a little bit put by in reserve, that my sister sends me in case of emergency, and then I hopped it.'

'Without telling anyone?'

'Of course without telling anyone. D'you think they'd have let me go?'

'Didn't you even get a coat . . . or a scarf?'

'No,' said Stephen. 'I forgot about those.'

'Wasn't there enough money to buy anything to eat?'

'Not after I'd bought my railway ticket. The trains in this country are fearfully expensive. In fact I was even a penny short for the ticket but the man at the booking office let me off. They can be awfully nice sometimes, especially the older ones. I know because I watch trains a lot . . .'

'But what about Slansky? Why did you have to hide when you got here?'

'That's just it. The beastly chauffeur must've tipped the old man the wink after all. For as I stepped off the train and on to the platform, what did I see? That same awful car again; and then I really had to run for it I can tell you. I ran down the railway line and straight into a tunnel . . .'

'Did nobody *see*?' exclaimed Alison excitedly.

'Only the *chauffeur*. This is the strangest thing. That man must have eyes in the side of his head. I knew he'd spotted me as soon as I stepped off the train because he started the car . . .'

'Oh crikey! But then did no one else see? . . . None of the railway staff?'

'No one. The train was still in the platform. They'd have

been after me otherwise. The railway company doesn't like that sort of thing. There are notices about it all over the place.'

'And at the other end of the tunnel?'

'Well, at the other end of the tunnel (luckily no trains came) there was no road either, which is a blessing, because they'd have got me if there had been one, I can tell you. I just set straight off for the ruins. I've been going there since I was a child so I knew roughly where they were. I used a landmark you know; a kind of folly up behind the school over there. You can't see it now because there's another hill in the way, and in any case it's too dark.'

It *was* dark. It was now so dark that they had to use the torch and Alison was frightened lest it might be seen, though if you thought calmly about it the possibility was not, after all, so *very* likely. The two men had the whole of the forest to choose from.

But she'd reckoned without the beady eyed chauffeur.

There was *indeed* something special about that man. When he'd presented himself to Slansky on the personal recommendation of one of the highest officials in the land, it had to be admitted the Count had not thought much of the rather slight and decidedly unostentatious figure. The work for which he was needed might be dangerous and, more importantly, required a certain accuracy of judgement if the mission was to succeed. One could never be sure with the English police for instance. Even their traffic laws were left handed. But the man had soon been fitted out with a uniform more suited to his status. As for himself . . . well, Stansky had never considered it worth hiding his own identity. He was too old and too well known for that sort of childish nonsense, and in any case the Count was a proud man.

He expected (and invariably got) every attention to detail and the comforts befitting his international status. Count Slansky was more used to state banquets and the official openings of war museums than this ignominious crawling about the countryside.

The Scotsman had turned out, sure enough, to know his job. Though he spoke little (in either a bastard English or more rapid Slav) he acted fast; and when it came to outwitting the police, well, he acted with the military precision that befitted his position as the most eminent traitor in the British army.

How Slansky hated *that* bunch of fools. They pretended to want to help his country, whilst all the time working subversively for the other side. By the 'other side' Slansky meant, of course, those underground movements who were now so alarmingly threatening the seat of power. That had *always* been their way. They were a two faced lot these British: as nice as pie to your face and then doing things behind your back only a Communist would dream of.

'Pouff.'

He spat out the word as, squatting uncomfortably on a damp mossy boulder behind a convenient tree, he awaited the coming of Miss Dayne, after her wretched ramblings to the nearby town.

He could not believe she would take such an odd route, or go quite so far, just to get a library book, but his chauffeur had insisted that this was the shortest way and that that was exactly what she was doing . . . and now blessed if he wasn't actually right.

For here in the semi-dusk *was* a little light . . . and not one schoolgirl, but two of them. Somewhere, somehow, she'd contrived to pick up a friend. Well, that, he allowed, was possible enough. Doubtless the other one had been out taking tea with some batty English relation and Alison Dayne had been sent to bring her back. But what an opportunity to get the brat and with a little gentle persuasion force her to divulge the whereabouts of the object he sought, that object he knew to be in her possession and that meant so much to his future. Indeed, it was only this bag or box – or rather what it contained – that stood between him and his continued existence in this world. There was no time now for such ugly thoughts. The voices were approaching and the man by his side had hold of his arm.

'Is it to be you, or me?' Slansky hissed.

'You,' said the other, without loosening his hold.

'I'm getting ready to jump out then.'

'Yes. You do that.'

'Well let go of my arm.'

'I'm just steadying you.'

'I don't need steadying.'

'Yes you do, or you might bungle it . . .'

Here were the two girls. In this faintest of lights one looked an odd creature in her spectacles but the other was Alison Dayne alright; he would swear to it, in spite of the hood. Instrument at the ready, he prepared for the spring. They were passing, talking in low tones, and he sprang. He found himself flat on his face. That fool chauffeur had *not* let go of his arm. Indeed he was still holding it – in a grip of steel, smiling blandly into the Count's own furious countenance.

'What did you have to do that for?'

The Count spat out the question with a viperous hiss. The children's voices were retreating, their owners having evidently heard nothing. Yet the cold steel had passed within a whisper of the Dayne girl's cheek.

'Two of them,' the Scotsman softly drawled. 'Anyway . . . she might not have been the same girl.'

'Of course she was,' the thwarted Count furiously spat out. 'You could see by the hair.'

'All right,' agreed the chauffeur, his voice suddenly hard, 'but I don't want to have to watch you disfigure a pretty face for nothing.' And disengaging the clutching fingers he forced the foreigner's weapon from their grasp.

The cut throat razor fell to the ground with a soft plop.

A pale moon had appeared and in the dark green moss the polished blade winked up at them evilly. They stared at it together for some time. Then the big bearded man looked up.

'You pig-headed, insubordinate fool,' he snarled. 'You call the Kyasht nothing?'

The unexpectedly strong chauffeur stood up with a sigh. 'You think she'd talk?' he enquired steadily. 'You'd get no more from her than from her father – you and your so called professionals. Let's waste no more time. We'd best be getting down to the school for there'll be something going on in that place quite soon that I'm badly wanting to see.'

The Count pulled himself together. He rose to his full height, and blew his nose, very loudly. Then he glanced again at this impudent Scotsman who had so suddenly taken the whole affair into his own hands.

There were visions going through his mind of overpowering the man. They only lasted a minute. His wrist still stung from that plier-like grip.

'Very well,' he said unsteadily, 'but let there be no question this time.'

'There'll be no question . . . never fear. You'll have Alison at your mercy and the Kyasht too, damn it—'

'You are sure?'

'I'm sure.'

'But how shall I foil her?'

'You'll think of a way when you're down there. You need never despair of that.'

There *was* something going on inside Miss Devine's study when Alison and Stephen passed by its window.

Usually by this time in the evening the curtains had been drawn on the cosy snug interior. Tonight they remained neglected and open. The drama in progress within was both vigorous and unequivocal. The voices were raised and the participants clearly visible.

Thankfully, with the rest of the school either doing prep or closeted inside their studies, Alison and Stephen, peering through the window, were the sole witnesses of the extra-ordinary display. Miss Devine sat, head in hands, with her back to them at her desk. Beyond her, a wild and unkempt figure paced the carpet, hiccuping and then breaking out again into passionate avowal.

'Yes, yes,' Miss Devine was urging pacifically, 'I have promised you Miss Prosser, have I not?'

'She's a *disgrace* – a disgrace to the school.'

Hat over one eye, coat mud stained and liberally hooked with briar, twig and fern, the agitated and almost unrecogniz-able second mistress momentarily advanced towards the window. The two ducked hastily out of sight. But the outpouring continued unabated as the mistress wheeled again, then paused to stamp her foot.

'She's a wicked, wicked girl. She had been gated and yet again she broke the bounds. Has she no shame? Has she no morals whatever that she can so flout authority?'

'She shall be punished,' assured the gentle but insistent voice of the Head, and Alison blanched in a chill of horror. Miss Devine had said she should be punished? She couldn't *mean* it? Surely she couldn't mean *that*?

Alison commanded the bewildered Stephen to stay where he was standing in the flower bed and then ran round the school. Prosser's voice sneered audibly:

'Pooh . . . what is the good? She has been punished time after time and what difference has it made? No . . . there is something repellent about her impudence that I cannot tolerate any longer. I must speak out . . .'

The second mistress swivelled round. There had been a knock at the door.

'Come in?'

Alison entered. Rather than stare at her, wide eyed and incredulous, she tried not to look at Miss Prosser at all.

'Ah,' cried the aggrieved mistress, her breast heaving. 'You are a contemptuous and insolent hussy, madam, and I demand your explusion forthwith!'

Alison gasped.

Expulsion?

She was to be expelled? This had, after all, been some trick?

'Certainly, if, when I know the facts . . .'

That Miss Devine was about to add something further was perfectly clear. But the Head was not allowed to add that further clarifying thing.

'The facts?' screeched Prosser, dramatically indicating her clothes. (And it had to be admitted her appearance was unusual.) 'Do not the facts stare you in the face?'

'Rest assured,' the Head continued calmly, still not looking at Alison, 'if it is proved that Alison did wrong, I shall not hesitate to impose punishment of the greatest severity.'

Here at last the Headmistress permitted her eyes to rest on Alison's own. It had been but for a moment, but long enough for the anxious fourteen year old. Alison imperceptibly sighed with relief. In those violet depths the message had been clear, and the Head was having as much difficulty controlling her inner excitement as was the girl herself.

'She *shall* be expelled?'

Without warning, the second mistress stretched out her hands. The Head gazed fascinated and repelled at the wiry fingers that now grasped her own.

'If necessary,' she found herself assuring the beseeching

figure, 'she shall be expelled.'

But now once having got hold of the desired and desirable object, Miss Prosser appeared to have no intention of ever letting it go again and the Head found herself physically backing away.

'Then in the meantime,' the grating voice was urging, with a smouldering glare at this creature too disgusting even to remain in the school, 'let her be removed from ordinary girls and made to sleep elsewhere.'

Now as it happened, nothing could have suited the Head's plan better. With the problem of hiding Stephen from the rest of the St Ursula's inmates, she had chosen a little-used room known with affection as the 'Old Girls' Dormitory'. Though certainly used by these 'Old Girls' when they came to the school to relive some of the terrors and deprivations of their time there, it was in the same wing as the sanitorium and, in fact, served to house the overflow at times of epidemic illness.

There were washbasins and a private bathroom. There were curtains that could be drawn on the world outside and a door with lock and bolts. Located as it was over Mr Brisling's boiler room, the place was also warm, and she had even spent the occasional night there herself. So she had chosen this ideal hiding place for her little brother now, away from those many girlish, inquisitive eyes that would soon otherwise be prying into their secret.

Alison too, to satisfy the wearying demands of her colleague, could be accommodated in the 'san' close by, at least for tonight, until she'd had a chance to clear her mind and start formulating some answers to a problem that had to be faced sooner or later, and whose ramifications were terrifying.

Let her at least be allowed to deal with one hurdle at a time. For Miss Devine still did not know whether the boy was safe. If only she could be rid of this embarrassing woman and discover whether Alison's mission had been successful. She jerked away her hand.

'Alison shall remain apart.' She could assure her injured rival on this one point anyway. 'In the Old Girls' Wing. You have my word.'

Just for a second, Miss Prosser permitted her satisfaction to show itself. Something almost resembling a smile crossed that harassed face. Then with a derisory sniff she swung on her heel and left the study. Miss Devine turned to her envoy with a beseeching smile.

'*Well* Alison?'

The girl pointed to the window.

'Look . . .'

'Stephen!'

The echoes of that heartfelt cry still rebound joyfully about the ancient cloisters of St Ursula's School for Girls. The thrill of their reunion was plain for Alison to see, and she didn't begrudge them a minute of it. In fact she was grinning all over her face during the whole soppy process. For it was only later, thinking about all that hugging, that her thoughts had slipped wistfully back to her own Daddy. Let us not dwell on such sadness. Because half an hour later was gathered together in the snugness of the lamplight a jollier company than the old wing had seen in many a long day.

The big panelled room was divided into cubicles, at least as far as the beds were concerned. So the party chose a window seat to sit on. And what a cheery gathering that was! Stephen in dressing gown and pyjamas now groaning that he couldn't eat another thing; Alison saying to Hilary, 'All right, well just one more then,' and popping yet another fabulous chocolate into her mouth. Miss Devine herself bustled about seeing to the bed and turning the taps on and off just in case there might have been a blockage in the pipes since yesterday.

At last they were all ready, four goggle eyed faces – three keenly expectant and one extremely bleary – gathered round their divine Headmistress. Miss Devine (or Nasy as Stephen called her – 'Such a romantic name,' Hilary sighed for ever after, 'Anast*asia*') settled down to her task.

'I suppose you dreadful girls want the truth?'

'Oh yes please Miss Devine.'

'The whole truth and nothing but the truth?'

'Yes . . . Yes, if that wouldn't be too much to ask.'

'Well, I promised, and you shall have it.'

Hilary wriggled. Stephen had closed his eyes, but opened them again because his name was being mentioned: 'Stephen here, contrary to appearances, is not an ordinary schoolboy.'

After this frank assertion, they all stared at him and the boy blinked back.

'No, we are half Bosnavian, Stephen and I, and members of an ancient house. My father, against the wishes of his uncle the old king, married a very plain English lady and was accordingly banished here to this country for ever. Our mother was very beautiful, but she was not of a noble line and so . . .'

'Did you say . . . *king*?' Hilary stammered. Her mouth had dropped open and she gazed uncomprehendingly into the beautiful face. ('Gawped,' Jennifer said afterwards. 'She literally gawped.')

'Why yes,' came the laughing reply. 'Our great uncle was the King of Bosnavia. When he became too old to govern, he appointed as Regent our half cousin, Igor. That man we now all know as . . . Count Slansky.'

'You mean *our* Slansky? That man actually rules Bosnavia?'

Hilary had never heard of the small Balkan kingdom, sandwiched between Bosnia and neighbouring Hercegovina, but she picked up the name quickly enough now.

'At this moment, certainly, he can be said to rule in a fashion. But only while there is no king on the throne. Ours is a mysterious land, topped by high mountains, where communication is difficult. Much money has been spent on armaments and the Secret Police, not so much on roads. The land is in some parts still virtually unexplored, with bears and wolves roaming the forests. So our people are poor. Their agriculture is backward. Since there is only one railway, they use mules to transport their produce to local markets. Always their movements are hampered by mountains. There is usually snow on the high passes. This makes it difficult for Slansky to collect his crippling taxes, but it has not been easy either for the people to organize any solid resistance. Now at last, with trouble in all the Balkans, we are in a state of massive revolt; and although Slansky's Secret Police shoot peasants – and their wives and children – every day, the people call for a *new* leader . . .'

'Not . . . Stephen?' Hilary asked incredulously.

'Yes,' laughed Miss Devine as the sagging boy, poked in the ribs by Jennifer, jerked back to life. 'Why ever not?'

Looking at him now, it might have been tempting to reply,

'Because he simply doesn't look like one.'

Leaders of nations are big men, with fierce moustaches and grey pointed beards – like the Count himself. Miss Devine however seemed unperturbed by their surprise.

'As the only living male heir to the throne, Stephen must emerge and accept his duty. His subjects will love their new king, just as they loved their old one. To restore the monarchy they will fight Slansky and his thugs with their bare hands. Don't worry, they have already begun. And with arms being sent in by more than twenty friendly nations – Britain being, needless to say, the friendliest – victory cannot be too far away. There remains yet one insuperable, and what may seem to modern girls like you rather silly, dilemma. You see, unlike you English, my people are simple and credulous. They have advanced not a whit, Heaven be praised, from the state of their fathers, and their fathers before that. It's what he's *used to* that counts in the peasant mind.'

'Go on,' said Alison, who was biting her nails.

'Well, since time immemorial, at the Coronation a certain ring has been placed on the third finger of the monarch's left hand. The act is one of magical significance. Without the ring there can be no ceremony, it is *so* important to the people (and therefore also to Stephen and myself). Now this same magic ring was until recently believed to be totally lost. Then quite miraculously it turned up again in the family vault of one of your oldest English houses. This may seem incredible, but your father, Alison, was instructed to bring that ring . . .'

Miss Devine was not allowed to continue. There was a massive interruption as Hilary started to her feet, ablaze with sudden enlightenment.

'The chocolates!' she cried. 'The little box!'

Then with a sigh she dropped to her knees and, gazing up into a laughing face, shook and shook her triumphant chum.

For Alison, all had now been explained, and she could produce her prize. Of course it had been Alison's hand that, a few hours previously, had delved in the soil under the great lily. She'd correctly guessed most of the story even then. Only its details awaited confirmation and Miss Devine had confirmed them now.

With a sigh of satisfaction she could simply dip her hand in her pocket and produce this thing that, with its glorious royal crest, was what the whole mystifying affair had been about. She'd have produced it earlier had she been clearer about a couple of things. But she had had to be sure; only now with (or so she thought) every single possible end tied up, could she hold out in her hand the precious object for all to see.

It was Miss Devine's turn to react.

'Alison,' she breathed. 'Alison . . . Alison Dayne; what *do* you have . . . ?'

Stephen wasted no time. He was in fact a good deal more practical than he may have at first sight appeared. At least he was a boy and practically all boys possess penknives. He found no difficulty in inserting its blade into the lock and after a few moments' manipulation had come a little 'click'. The box was open!

Inside lay a gold ring inlaid with silver. But what was more important, on the crest of that ring sat a diamond every bit as big as a threepenny piece. In fact the glittering object was like nothing so much as a rather vulgar prize in front of a coconut shy at the fairground. Had there ever been a diamond more huge? Not a real one, gloated Hilary and Jennifer together. The Head had taken the jewel and was staring transfixed at its hypnotizing brightness.

Every day, unlike Alison, she had been expecting to hear from Colonel Dayne the news that everything was fine, that the ring had been safely delivered to those trusty friends in the Bosnavian capital. But like Alison, she had heard nothing, and had begun, after all, to fear everything lost. On that day in the study with Alison, after Slansky had first made his appearance, a knell of doom had sounded, and the distraught young woman had wondered if after all both Stephen and Alison's father, too, might be dead. Yet, since the Dictator had appeared in person, there must be some other reason. And now she knew what that reason was.

'The Kyasht!' she burst out in an immensity of relief, 'the "Imp" himself!' Without the ring there could be no Coronation. Slansky knew that as well as she did. His continuing oppression would have been assured – but now . . .

'Oh my dear Alison.'

She was squeezing and hugging that embarrassed child with

a soft impetuousness that brought tears to the mild grey eyes of her charge, and a wonderful ache to an extremely susceptible heart. Gravely, Hilary shook her golden locks.

'Ali you know – you really are the tops . . .'

The twinsome two were gazing at their friend with the awe and reverence usually reserved for that other goddess who was at this moment clapping the Kyasht to her lips and then flinging it into the air in a way so un-English as to be almost *foreign*. This was the unbelievable thing. Their own revered Headmistress had actually been a foreigner all this time – a Royal one certainly, but a foreigner nevertheless – and they'd not even guessed!

'Keeping it to yourself all this time,' Jennifer chided Alison. 'We're amazed, aren't we Hil?'

'Dazzled beyond belief, old fraud.'

There came a thump on the floor. Stephen had just fallen off his seat with tiredness.

'It's been an ordeal for him,' said Miss Devine, setting her brother on his feet again and inadvertently pushing aside the curtains in the process. 'But you're *all right now*,' she assured him firmly.

'Am I Nasy? Am I really safe?'

Through the temporarily uncurtained window, he peered nervously into the yard. No. It was all right. There was no one there that he could see. They propped him up then half pushed, half carried him to his bed.

Completely unaware of the horrors to come, they gathered round the exhausted boy to bid him good-night. Just as the others were leaving Alison returned to Stephen's bedside.

'Stephen?'

'Yes?' came the sleepy reply.

'Do you want to be King?'

The boy became for a moment fully awake. He knit his brows.

'I don't know,' he answered truthfully. 'It's all so sudden I haven't even considered. If *you* were there, Alison, I don't think I'd mind anything any more . . .'

There was a slightly longer pause then.

'Stephen?' came the careful and considering voice again. 'Do *you* think I'm all those things Miss Prosser said?'

This time, the boy actually sat up.

'Oh Alison,' he declared vehemently, 'I think you're the nicest, the kindest and . . . and the prettiest girl I've ever seen.'

Not that he'd been allowed to see many, poor chap. Slowly he was relapsing on to his pillow again and in a moment came a steady breathing. Alison crept to the door and silently the three friends and their beloved Headmistress tip-toed down the corridor to the 'san'. Overcome with tiredness, Alison allowed herself to be tucked up between the crisp, white sheets. Almost before her friends had left she too had drifted effortlessly into sleep.

CHAPTER 15

Count Slansky's opinion of his chauffeur had suffered a meteoric decline during the last couple of hours. He was not used to being so treated by minions. The fact that, but for that particular lackey's swift action, Alison's face would have been marked for life mattered little to such a hardened and cold blooded campaigner. To the Count, such trivia were commonplace. Insubordination most definitely was not.

As they tramped, the two of them, back to the school, the big man in the queer flopping hat growled savagely to himself. Normally he could have worked off his feelings by having some peasant's ears removed. Or perhaps a lit cigarette stubbed out in somebody's eye. Now he could do neither of these things. For the slender Scotsman was unlikely to take kindly to such treatment and Slansky was beginning to wish he had never hired the man.

The possibility that the notorious murderer Colonel Harry Dayne had really handed over the Kyasht to his daughter in a box of chocolates had seemed to the Count a very long shot indeed. For the Colonel stood among the most respected and feared of all his enemies. Such folly was unlikely, to say the least. Had all this then been a wild goose chase? Not according to his Chief of Police.

Chosen by his Chief of General Staff – an old friend named Slibine Novotsky (a man he could *really* trust) – the chauffeur, it had to be admitted, had had, up till now, an uncanny knack of proving himself right.

He had clung to his quarry like a limpet, tailing the girl with a doggedness that suggested an almost personal obsession. That was the sort of keenness the Bosnavian Regent liked in his employees. Few foreigners, too, spoke his own tongue with such ease. Though perhaps not all important, that in itself was almost sufficient recommendation. Certainly it made life a lot easier for the Count.

Engineered as it had been entirely by his accomplice, the lead – up to the moment of denouement had been brilliant, masterly. And then had come this. The man had deliberately thwarted his *own* efforts; and all for a pretty face. Was the fool in love with a schoolgirl? To Slansky it seemed not only madness, but the loss of the first real opportunity they'd so far had. Wouldn't talk? The idea was ludicrous. Of course she'd talk. They always talked, such little sluts. And time was running out. By now the Prince would doubtless be on his way to Bosnavia under British protection. Without the Kyasht to dismantle and sell off to the highest bidder, Slansky knew his own regime was doomed. He would give the man one more chance. If he once again failed to come up with the goods, then 'kaput'. It was curtains for the sad Scotsman. Count Slansky would personally see to it that the fool was put down with the iron boot at the first available opportunity.

It was in this frame of mind that Slansky had at last been allowed to tramp into the school yard. It had taken some time to get there. First they'd had to watch some pantomime with the Devine woman and her second in command (that terrifying creature) and then Alison Dayne. As if *that* had any bearing on the all important quest.

And even from this ludicrous display of female temperament he'd found himself being suddenly dragged away, as if the whole host of Bosnavian vampires were at their heels. Now they were standing under some dimly lighted upper chamber and beside a small, almost subterranean cavern that housed a massive boiler glowing with angry coke.

Having tried the door and found it locked, the chauffeur was testing window catches and presently signalled that he'd found one open. The idea was for the Scotsman to enter the school alone. He would then creep to some place where, he swore, at this time of night the Dayne girl was bound to be found and there deliver the fateful letter from her 'father'. That this 'letter' was now squashed and damp was an advantage, since it would be more difficult to detect the obvious forgery from such a screwed up note. And then, just as the Count had resigned himself to another tedious vigil in the car under the rhododendrons . . . the miracle occurred!

That it was bad luck for Stephen will not be denied. For the Count it came as a godsend. For it was at that moment that the heir to the throne of Bosnavia accidently showed himself to the outside world. Face softly lit in the glow of a lamp, the bespectacled features were unmistakable. Slansky almost expired.

'It's him,' he croaked. 'It's the boy himself!'

For a moment the chauffeur seemed nonplussed. Then he slowly straightened.

'So? What do you intend to do?'

'Why – kill him of course. We've lost the ring and time is running out. I'm going to kill the boy.'

'Don't be stupid,' the chauffeur sneered. 'You could have done that a dozen times over.'

'But never to look like an accident.' The Count laughed softly. 'No one can blame Slansky for an accident. Get inside the building. Go up there and lock the door.'

The Scotsman shrugged his shoulders and did as he was bid.

The Count meanwhile walked rapidly towards the rhododendrons then broke into a run.

In a little while he emerged into the lane on the other side of those thick bushes and, peering about, attempted to find his car. It would be just typical now to find he had lost his own car, simply because that fool chauffeur had hidden it too well. After a few moments' running up and down the lane, he became panic stricken. Someone had stolen it. The whole plan was about to be ruined again just because . . . Then he caught sight of a brass lamp and plunged into the undergrowth.

On the running boards of such powerful open touring cars is often strapped a gallon can of petrol, held in position by a leather strap. This the Count undid with shaking fingers. Would the can be full? Relief! It was full to the brim. The Count seized the handle with a gutteral exclamation and set off back along the track with the heavy can. He soon felt quite exhausted. Hot and tired, Slansky was snarling as he staggered into the yard. They were a bunch of twisting, double crossing, untrustworthy villians in his country!

Oh, it was a thankless task being a dictator, he reflected, as he searched in his pocket for the box of matches the chauffeur had so quietly removed just ten minutes earlier. No matter. This boiler would serve.

He had at last spread the whole contents of the can all around the room and over the walls and now fashioned a taper from one of Mr Brisling's old sandwich papers. Seizing hold of the boiler door and then clamping back his yell of agony, he flung open the orifice and released a blast of heat that quite seered his nose. In a trice the whole place was suddenly ablaze and Slansky stepped hastily back, activating some feudal enemy device that immediately rendered him unconscious. What he'd done of course (Mr Brisling being a gardener) was to step on a rake. The thing rose up to smack him in exactly the right spot between the eyes, where that particularly important nerve is, and the large body of Bosnavia's unpopular ruler slowly zigzagged, crumpled, then fell. It slumped half in and half out of the door of the blazing room, with the consequence that part of him was rather cooked (the bottom end) while the top (the dangerous end) survived more or less unscathed.

Normally at that time of the evening the old porter and sweeper of dead leaves would have been found with his legs propped up beside the boiler, a glass of porter conveniently to his hand. With his small but ferocious Jack Russell terrier sitting meekly beside him, the scene would be a tranquil one, a nice painting subject for some local country artist. Tonight things were different. As luck would have it, Towser the School Dog had only that day gone visiting. He'd departed on his annual holiday with Mr Brisling's fat old sister, who once a year liked to take the animal to the seaside so that it might romp with a few friends around the sandy beach and tear up fish and chip papers. Deprived of his trusty companion, Mr Brisling had taken himself to the Dog and Duck to drown his sorrows, and he has never ceased to regret that fact.

Even then, guilt had quickly brought him back to his post only to find the boiler room ablaze and a man climbing through the library window. He dispatched the chauffeur quickly enough, with a handy shovel. But it was this fire that even now threatened to wipe out all traces of his beloved boiler house that so perturbed the old gardener.

Passing a hand over a creased and bewildered brow, he was

round the corner of the building with the speed of a fireman sliding down a greasy pole, yelling for dear life:

'Fire! Fire!'

'Brisling! What's going on?'

Miss Devine had stuck her head from a study window.

'There's a fire my lady! Ring the Brigade!' And before she could question him further the ancient man had vanished in search of a hose.

The Head instantly did as she was bid, knowing the importance of speed on these occasions. At first she had great difficulty in getting through since all the firemen were in the pub. Even though she jabbed the instrument up and down rapidly, she could not make contact. It had not yet occurred to her to connect this event in any way with Stephen. 'Hello?' she was calling urgently. 'Hello? Is there anyone there? Ah . . . thank goodness. Yes. This is St Ursula's School for Girls and we've apparently got a fire . . .' The receiver had gone down and now her first thought must be for her girls and mistresses. Fire drill . . . that was the thing! A bell was already being rung.

It was this bell that awoke Alison. At first she fancied she'd been dreaming. But then came other sounds within the school and the switching on of lights everywhere. There was a strange trembling sound beneath the floor. Then she screamed. For issuing through the bare floor boards close to the window came an unmistakable coil of smoke. She lay transfixed for a moment. Her eyes lifted to the window. A licking tongue of smokey flame had at that moment flickered past the glass and she was out of her bed in a trice.

'Stephen! Stephen!' she yelled, wrenching open the door of her room and hurling herself along the corridor to Stephen's room. Convulsively she shook the heavily sleeping form. 'You've got to wake up! There's a fire!'

The boy sat up in bed. His first thought was for his spectacles and he groped around in the semi-darkness on the locker top. But then he found and rammed the lenses on his nose.

'Alison? What are *you* doing here?'

The girl turned back in despair. For smoke had begun to fill this room too and lay in a sullen coiling cloud suspended between floor and ceiling. She was coughing as she ran to the door dragging Stephen out into the corridor as she went. In seconds they'd reached the door connecting the 'san' wing with the rest of the building. She tried the handle.

There seemed to be somebody simultaneously twisting it on the other side and shouting in a muffled voice:

'Alison! Oh Alison . . . unlock the door! There's a fire.'

It was Hilary.

'I can't,' Alison yelled back frantically. 'There isn't a key.'

'Well there's nothing here either. Can't you get Stephen to break down the door?'

Now Stephen too lent his full weight and they crashed together into the solid oak panels. The door gave hardly a shudder as the two battering rams retired with bruised shoulders.

'It's no good Hil,' Alison wailed. 'You'll just have to run and get help.'

As she heard the footsteps go scrambling off downstairs again, she gazed round for some other means of escape. She ran back to the window of Stephen's room. She could see a sea of white faces gazing up at her. The whole school seemed to be gathered out there on the grass and they mostly screamed: 'Alison! Alison! . . .' and did very little else. An antique hose could be seen lying snaked across the grass but there was difficulty connecting it to the water supply and the flames were now really roaring.

Already the old 'san' felt intolerably hot. Stephen was groping hopelessly at the door. Alison darted to the bed. By standing on one end she managed to tear the tough cotton sheet in two. Then with shaking hands she tore it into strips, jabbing one into a jug of water and wrapping it round her mouth, and then plunging in another. The boy king was already sagging as she hauled him into the room with her. While she wrapped the wet cloth round his mouth, she watched, mesmerized, a little tongue of evil, exploratory flame creep out and have a good peer round the room. 'Yes; it's all right lads,' she could just hear it saying . . . 'you can come up now.'

'Miss Devine,' she screamed, 'where are you?'

There was no reply. At that moment came a gigantic crash

and the oak door shuddered in its frame.

'The stairs have collapsed,' somebody was shouting below.

Alison bit her nails. Her father would not be content to hang around like this, waiting to be charred to a cinder. Through the gap in the floor flames now issued . . . some of the real flames that could be heard roaring and chattering below. Great Heavens, there must be something she could do? Her companion was rapidly failing and lay in a torpor on the floor. Alison's own lungs were good, but she could not hold out much longer.

'Help,' she feebly gasped, beating her hands on the panelling for no logical reason. 'Help! Help!' And then it was that from infinitely far away came the voice of persistent memory, repeating some really worn out phrase just over and over again as though from the end of a gramophone record.

There's even a secret passage, came the voice of her father. *You just press a hidden button in the panel* . . .

Oh mercy! A section of floor gave way with a rending crash, sending up a shower of sparks. Blindly, feverishly, Alison's hands were slithering over those smoothly polished sections of oak that stood between her and her freedom. If only . . . Pray God it wasn't some story; some sad little tale concocted just to make her feel better at the time. The smoke was so thick she could hardly see, the heat savage, blistering the paintwork over on the window sills.

Blindly she worked on. She was instinctively breathing fresh air that seemed to come from a crack in the woodwork; and then suddenly, compulsively, going to that place herself . . . in a way that was entirely instinctive, falling, sliding, collapsing down that rough and cold hewn stone till she scraped the flesh from her hands. And it was this that brought her struggling to her feet. Rushing back through the inferno of the room to haul a corpse-like figure from the flames and into this dark cool sympathetic chamber of non-inflammable stone, and then bump, bump, bump, down stone steps, slimy with long disuse. Down and down, seemingly for ever.

At last the blessed cool of damp grass.

And now Hilary's excited and relieved voice:

'Oh you precious and quite ludicrous old thing! You came out of a queer little slit in the wall right down at ground level

114

and hidden behind a great unpruned evergreen. I only spotted you myself by chance; but by the time I did, you'd managed to haul Stephen right out and were staggering about like anything . . . like somebody drunk I s'pose. Then you fell and collapsed in my arms and I yelled: "Miss Devine. She's all right. She's here . . ."'

And Miss Devine came running. Everyone came running and Stephen was being knelt by and fanned and at that moment . . .

CHAPTER 16

'*December 14th, 1931 . . .*

At that moment I felt consciousness ebbing away. Daddy, you must be wondering at this great gap in the log and I s'pose I'll have to tell you sometime. I burnt my hand you see just a teeny bit. There won't be a scar or anything but I've had it bandaged until today and I haven't even been able to write any lessons. To be truthful, that hasn't worried your only daughter too much; in fact rather the reverse, especially since Prosey's gone. You'll never believe this but on the night of the fire she simply disappeared and hasn't been seen since. There must be a reason but it's difficult to think of one.

Hil and Jen of course claim she was in league with Slansky all the time. I know that can't be true. So what's the old beezum up to? Though I've been racking my brains (such as they are) I still haven't come up with an answer. The official explanation is that she's entered a state of well earned retirement; but schoolmistresses don't just suddenly do that, do they? Usually they wait till the end of term.

Anyhow, what an incredible night that was for all of us. You will be relieved to hear that the fire was eventually brought under control and thankfully only a few rooms were seriously damaged. One of the night's heroes incidentally was Maud, who manned one of the pumps. Since then she seems to have had a complete change of heart, and now no one could be nicer or more reasonable. I suppose the fire sobered everyone *down. In fact everything has ended up well for everybody—*' and here came a smudge on the page – '*everyone that is (and Daddy I've got to say this) except me.*' There was another smudge. '*Daddy, it really is the end of*

116

my first term here. Tomorrow there's the carol service and then all the other girls go home. I suppose I should be feeling really Christmassy. In fact I'm rather miz . . . '

If you will recollect or simply turn back to the beginning of this book, you will note that these lines were not the last of this particular day's entry in Alison's interrupted 'log'.

Indeed, she had a great deal more to tell her father, and not merely about her present state of mind and the feelings of gnawing worry that had eventually actually paralysed the poor little hand that was really still quite sore, and had begun to ache again quite badly after all the scribbling.

So she paused, pen in mouth. Staring hard into the common room fire, looking at the holly and at the snow falling softly outside, she wondered what exactly she *should* be thinking of her father's promise to be back by the Christmas holidays. Well . . . it hadn't actually *been* a promise, she supposed miserably. That was the trouble with her father's job. He could never guarantee anything.

Just then the door burst open and Hilary bounced in. She plumped down on the arm of the easy chair beside Alison, and as the girl's watering eyes looked anxiously up the best chum of all enquired in the gentlest of voices:

'All alone?' The tear stained face managed a wan smile at that solicitous observation, so Hilary added, 'I should think that diary's long enough to turn into a book by now.'

There was no point in keeping the truth dark any longer.

'Oh; it's just for my Dad really; to make up for all the letters I never wrote.'

A frisson of supressed excitement passed across the other girl's cheery, pink-cheeked countenance.

'It *has* been the most incredible term. You must have the idea school's always like this. Just wait until next year.'

'Yes,' Alison agreed ruefully. 'When the work *truly* has to start.'

'At least Prossy won't be here.'

'Poor old thing,' Alison murmured. 'I do feel sorry for her.'

'She should never have submitted to that blind hatred, my angel one,' came the sage reply. 'Anyway, it was time she had a rest from us.' There came a pause, then: 'I wonder what your Stephen's doing now?'

'He's not *my* Stephen.'

'He's nobody else's,' Hilary laughed gaily. 'I haven't noticed any of us being invited over to Bosnavia. I can't say I'm rapturous about him being a king. He'll get terribly spoiled. But with the jolly old Count still as stiff as a banana in his hospital bed – well, there doesn't seem any other way out of it. And then,' she added lightly, 'you'll be Queen.'

Nothing could have been more mocking than that plummy voice. Alison half rose.

'Hilary Marchant,' she declared, batting her friend over the head with her diary. But there was no time to continue the discussion, for here were Jennifer and Maud silently ranging themselves in front of her, their hands clasped and their heads held back in the strangest . . . *deference*. Really, there was no other word for it. In fact it was the queerest kind of arrangement altogether, for as though at some pre-arranged sign Hilary walked to join them; as if she'd been waiting for them all the time, and now that they'd come in, had only to nod and agree with whatever it was they intended to say.

Jennifer cleared her throat.

'Ali,' she began, and then coughed. 'Ali. Maud's got something to divulge.'

'You tell her . . .'

'No . . . come on. Don't be a goose.'

'Alison. Miss Devine wants you in carol practice right away.'

Stiffly, the three of them then turned. Like geese, they filed quietly from the room.

Well, here was a rummy go indeed. A frown had clouded Alison's brow, and she blinked. But she laid down her notebook, and having given her nose a good blow followed the others across the hall and into the the big oak clad music room with its minstrel's gallery and the enormous Christmas tree reaching right up to the ceiling.

Carol practice was what Alison had been instructed to attend. Up until a few moments ago the cheerful sound of Christmas music had filled the air. But at this suspended moment, a peculiar silence hung over the sea of expectant faces.

Alison found herself being urged forward to a place beside

118

the fire and under the great pine that, covered with festive candles, reached upward so gracefully and with such dignity. It seemed to be remembering that lonely forest above St Ursula's from which it had come.

'We had adventures there,' it was whispering and Alison nodded, as all those about her waited and watched. Those adventures! Miss Devine too seemed to be poignantly recalling memories as she gazed into the abstracted face.

'Girls,' she began without taking her eyes off Alison's face. 'I have already had occasion to thank Alison publicly for her unprecedented act of heroism in the recent fire . . .'

They watched and waited. The embers' glow spread to Alison's cheeks.

'But for her inspired efforts, I would now be deprived of a schoolgirl comrade, a well loved brother, and Bosnavia would be deprived of its rightful king. Yet this is history. What none of you will know is the role that Alison's *father*, Colonel Harry Dayne, has played in that poor country of mine, so ravaged by strife.' As Miss Devine threw her a triumphant signal, Alison bit her lip. 'Acting under orders from a friendly Britain, and together with the new hugely successful "populist" party, the Colonel has been engaged in a desperate struggle to regain control over a corrupt army and establish a new elected government. Two days ago, I am delighted to report, this aim was finally achieved! And now Alison, to the really thrilling news. Your father . . .'

As Miss Devine gestured broadly towards the gallery, all eyes turned with her.

It was a moment of great tension. They knew Alison's plight. They'd been unable even to say 'sorry' about what must feel the most beastly of all beastlinesses – not knowing whether your nearest and most dear person was even alive. Now their hearts were in their mouths. A figure stepped forward; there came a united gasp, not of relief, unfortunately, but the most frightful shock. For it was not after all Colonel Dayne, or anyone remotely resembling that unmistakable army man.

The individual who stood up there looking down at them was an ordinary leather uniformed chauffeur, and *how* sourly he surveyed them all from his eyrie. What on earth could be

119

happening? In dismayed, utter disbelief, Alison gaped at Hil and Jen. No sign of life animated those usually vivid faces. From everyone else had come a cry of disappointment and Alison had felt her stomach drop.

But even as they gazed up at the figure he was contriving somehow to *take off his face*, completely to remove it, with his spectacles, his scowl and his moustache disappearing all in one go. And there, struggling out of his leather coat, was an impertinently grinning Colonel Dayne. It was her father! It had been her father *the whole time*. For a moment Alison struggled, paralysed in the grip of surging emotion, then:

'Daddy!' she shrieked, in almost one bound reaching the bottom of the gallery steps, and then, meeting him half way, she threw herself into the arms of this oh-so-loved and impeccably uniformed British army officer. 'Oh Daddy . . . I might have known!'

And indeed she might, had she tried to imagine that far ahead, have guessed that the Colonel could, all long, have been up to his old tricks. Secret disguises; the illusion of the commonplace; turning into the impossible, just when you least expected it – such of course were the tools of his trade. But that he should have been actually *with* her all that time – oh, it was almost too much to bear! Triumphantly she led him by the hand down into the midst of the surging throng. He kissed her this time, again and again.

'You can be proud of your daughter, Harry,' Miss Devine was shouting above the din all round. 'She's a true Dayne!'

The Colonel clasped as many of the reaching hands as he could touch, then shook his head.

'I shudder to think how she might have been a very *dead* true Dayne – thanks to my stupidity on that railway platform.'

For most of those present the display they'd been promised was now over, and at a nod from Miss Devine they trooped dutifully from the room, an excitedly chattering throng of schoolgirls – the best in the world. But Hilary and Jennifer were not allowed to escape so easily. Together with Alison they formed a truly triumphant trio and they were not going to be allowed to forget it. They'd been in since the start, and Alison now clutched them to her just as fiercely as she held her father.

'But Daddy? What about *you*?' she enquired earnestly,

gazing into his face. 'Did they hurt you, those awful foreign people at the station? For they must have thought you still had the little box . . .'

'Certainly a couple of agents had a go at me on the London train. Didn't get much change.' The Colonel laughed. He'd probably overcome the lot of them single handed, if the truth were known. Oh, he was so rash and debonair – so romantic! How lucky she was to have such a father. How proud she was to show him off to the others whose enlarged eyes all told the same envious story. 'It was that chap with the camera that spoiled things.' The Colonel frowned with remorseful memory. 'I *instantly* realized what a fool deed I'd done, putting the Kyasht with those chocolates. It slipped in so easily you see. Oh Lord. I'm sorry! I'd no idea how many of them there were. There might have been a dozen fully armed professional soldiers. As it happened, what they boiled down to were just six incompetent nitwits and I was able to throw them off easily. I *knew* the thing'd be safer with you than anyone else in the world, but I put you in a pretty foul position and oh, how it nagged and nagged away at my conscience! So when I heard on the grapevine that Slansky had finally decided to pop over here himself, I offered the chap my personal services.'

The gollys, the ahs and oohs, the significant looks exchanged, indicated just how much thrilling gossip there'd be to begin next term. One very important question however had been puzzling Alison for some time. So far, there'd been no mention of the famous fire and she wanted the answer to an enigma that really rather hurt.

'Daddy,' she asked anxiously. 'If you were *with* Slansky when he started the fire, why didn't you come and rescue me?'

'Oh golly love – I was *coming* to get you. But then, just as I was trying to shin up through an open window, someone hit me smartly over the head.'

'I *see*,' Alison breathed, as if an immense load had been taken from her mind.

It was Miss Devine's turn to speak. The Headmistress had so far said nothing. She'd laughed and sighed as much as anyone during the explanations. But at last must come the awful revelation that would provide the answer to what was probably the most tormenting question of all. She drew in her breath.

'It was Miss Prosser who locked the door.'

'Oh no!' gasped the 'twins'.

The Colonel was frowning. He noisily tapped his fingers on the mantelpiece. He had already heard this news. Now that they, too, understood, the quietness of death fell on the company. Uncertainly Hilary and Jennifer glanced at their chum. She had gulped. She almost turned away. But then Alison decided to face up to the truth.

'Miss Prosser couldn't bear me Daddy you see,' she explained. 'It must have been because she wanted to make sure I didn't pollute the other girls. She thought I was to be expelled, only I wasn't. She didn't understand . . .'

'She'll *never* forgive herself,' Miss Devine added unhappily. 'I haven't the slightest idea where she's gone. I just wish I did know; then we could all forgive and forget.'

'Humppp.' All that was as may be. The Colonel had noisily cleared his throat and *Alison* knew it was time to change the subject.

'But where have you been *since* the fire?'

The anxious faces relaxed again.

'Had to slip quietly back to Bosnavia, darling. A lot of work to be done . . .'

'But Colonel Dayne,' Hilary now burst out at last. 'Couldn't you have stopped old Slansky from doing his fell act? I mean, if you were with the man all that time, couldn't you have just . . . stopped him?'

'Dashed awkward actually Hilary.' The Colonel's brow wrinkled in perplexity. 'It would have meant at some stage I'd have had to kill him you see. There'd have been a quite furious international row. Not a British prerogative to get quite *so* involved. No. I reckoned that so long as I just stuck it out – glued myself to the man as it were . . .'

'*No*. I'm talking about the fire . . .'

'Because if it hadn't been for what you revealed about the secret panel . . .' Jennifer added accusingly.

'Yes, you remember Daddy?' Alison confirmed in an unsteady voice. 'On the Manor lawn the night before I came to school?'

122

The Colonel could be seen to gulp. He and the Head-mistress exchanged shamefaced glances.

'Golly,' broke in Hilary, tactful and warm hearted to the last. 'Let's have no more of such spooky thoughts. Good Heavens! This day, of all most joyous days, must not be spoiled. All's well that ends well. Because now, Ali, you'll be going home instead of having to spend Christmas here all alone.'

'I'd have said, of course, stay with me,' Miss Devine added penitently, 'if I'd not known your father was so desperately trying to get back in time.'

'Why don't you come with *us* Anastasia?' The Colonel spoke eagerly, impulsively and with a reddening face. 'Come with us to the Manor for Christmas.'

Was it the nearness of the fire? Or could there be some other explanation? An answering flush had most certainly appeared on that usually so pale cheek.

'I would love to come with you to the Manor for Christmas,' replied Miss Devine, delightedly.

'Oh Hil . . . isn't everything *wonderful*?' Alison suddenly exploded.

Amidst an answering roar of approval, Hilary decisively stuck up her hand.

'Girls. Girls. Let's have three rousing cheers – three of the most ear shattering yells for the most sporting, the most ripping, the most perfect Headmistress a school ever had! Hip hip . . .'

'Hooray!' rang out the answering cry, echoing away across those snowy wastes with their icy streams and frozen ponds, and all the wild places that had now returned to solitude . . .

'Hip hip, hooray!'

Fiction from Granada in paperback.

Holly Hobbie Richard Dubleman   £1.25 ☐
The exciting adventures of Liz Dutton who, with her magical friend
Holly Hobbie, wrestles with the dangers of the Guatemalan jungle to
save her father.

Ivory City Marcus Crouch   95p ☐
A collection of Indian folk tales.

The Trumpeter of Krakov Agnes Szudek   85p ☐
A collection of Polish folk tales.

War of the Computers Granville Wilson   85p ☐
A.D. 2010 and a global war breaks out between the computers which
govern Earth.
The Terror Cubes   85p ☐
A.D. 2050 and renegade robots threaten to take over Mankind's
society.

Trebizon Series Anne Digby
First Term at Trebizon   85p ☐
Second Term at Trebizon   95p ☐
Summer Term at Trebizon   85p ☐
Boy Trouble at Trebizon   95p ☐
More Trouble at Trebizon   85p ☐
The Tennis Term at Trebizon   85p ☐
Summer Camp at Trebizon   95p ☐
Into the Fourth at Trebizon   95p ☐
An exciting new modern school series about Rebecca Mason and
her five friends at boarding school.

The Big Swim of the Summer Anne Digby   60p ☐
Sara seems all set to win the big swimming race until she gets
involved with the strange new girl at Hocking School.

Bambi's Children Part One Felix Salten   60p ☐
Bambi's Children Part Two   60p ☐
Fifteen Rabbits   65p ☐
Three books of classic and much loved animal stories.

Shadows in the Pit Robin Chambers   70p ☐
A tense and exciting science fiction adventure.

Fiction from Granada in paperback.

The Adventures of Niko   Jonathan Rumbold   £1.25   ☐
The outrageous adventures of Niko, a Greek village boy.

Ben and Blackbeard   T.R. Burch   £1.25   ☐
Ben discovers a thief using his own favourite haunt by the river and
determines to capture the man single handed.

Young Sherlock: The Mystery of the Manor House
   Gerald Frow   95p   ☐
The first book of a new television series about Sherlock Holmes as a
17 year old just beginning his famous career as a detective.

Annie   Thomas Meehan   £1.25   ☐
The long-famous story of the New York orphan as related in the
musical of that name.

The Indian in the Cupboard   Lynne Reid Banks   £1.25   ☐
A toy Indian comes to life and makes great demands on his young
owner.
I, Houdini   £1.25   ☐
The adventures of a self-educated hamster.

Activity and Non-fiction Books from Granada.

Peter Eldin		
Match Play	85p	☐
Weston/Spooner		
Oxford Children's Dictionary	£2.95	☐
Richard Garrett		
File on Spies	95p	☐
File on Forgers	95p	☐
Jailbreakers	£1.25	☐
Margaret Crush		
Handy Homes for Creepy Crawlies	95p	☐

Verse and Rhyme from Granada

Deborah Manley (ed)		
Funny Poems	85p	☐
Cyril Fletcher (ed)		
Odes and Ends	90p	☐
Jennifer Mulherin (ed)		
Old Fashioned Nursery Rhymes	£1.25	☐

All these books are available at your local bookshop or newsagent, or can be ordered direct from the publisher.

To order direct from the publisher just tick the titles you want and fill in the form below.

Name _____

Address _____

Send to:
Dragon Cash Sales
PO Box 11, Falmouth, Cornwall TR10 9EN.

Please enclose remittance to the value of the cover price plus:

UK 45p for the first book, 20p for the second book plus 14p per copy for each additional book ordered to a maximum charge of £1.63.

BFPO and Eire 45p for the first book, 20p for the second book plus 14p per copy for the next 7 books, thereafter 8p per book.

Overseas 75p for the first book and 21p for each additional book.

Granada Publishing reserve the right to show new retail prices on covers, which may differ from those previously advertised in the text or elsewhere.